"You Little Devil!"

"I told you not to call me little," she reminded him with a smile and another spurt from the spray nozzle.

He leaned over the hood of the car and grabbed the nozzle from her.

"Let's quit and call it even, Nick. You never used to hold a grudge," she reminded him, backing away.

"I don't hold a grudge. I get even."

Melissa squeezed her eyes shut, expecting him to soak her. Instead she felt his lips brushing hers. "The old biddies are spying on us," he whispered. "Let's give them something to look at, shall we?" Without waiting another second, he settled his warm lips on hers, and Melissa forgot they were only supposed to be putting on a show....

Dear Reader,

This month it seems like everyone's in romantic trouble. We have runaway brides and jilted grooms....They've been left at the altar and wonder if they'll *ever* find true love with the right person.

Of course they do, and we get to find out how, as we read Silhouette Desire's delightful month of "Jilted!" heroes and heroines.

And what better way to start this special month than with *The Accidental Bridegroom*, a second 1994 *Man of the Month* from one of your favorites, Ann Major? I'm sure you'll enjoy this passionate story of seduction and supposed betrayal as much as I do.

And look for five more fabulous books by some of your most beloved writers: Dixie Browning, Cait London, Raye Morgan, Jennifer Greene and Cathie Linz. Yes, their characters might have been left at the altar...but they don't stay single for long!

So don't pick and choose—read about them all! I loved these stories, and I'm sure you will, too.

Lucia Macro
Senior Editor

Please address questions and book requests to:
Silhouette Reader Service
U.S.: 3010 Walden Ave., P.O. Box 1325, Buffalo, NY 14269
Canadian: P.O. Box 609, Fort Erie, Ont. L2A 5X3

CATHIE LINZ
BRIDAL BLUES

SILHOUETTE *Desire®*
Published by Silhouette Books
America's Publisher of Contemporary Romance

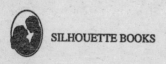 SILHOUETTE BOOKS

ISBN 0-373-05894-2

BRIDAL BLUES

Printed in U.S.A.

Books by Cathie Linz

Silhouette Desire

Change of Heart #408
A Friend in Need #443
As Good as Gold #484
Adam's Way #519
Smiles #575
Handyman #616
Smooth Sailing #665
Flirting with Trouble #722
Escapades #804
Midnight Ice #846
Bridal Blues #894

Silhouette Romance

One of a Kind Marriage #1032

CATHIE LINZ

was in her mid-twenties when she left her career in a university law library to become a full-time writer of contemporary romantic fiction. *Bridal Blues* is this bestselling Chicago author's twenty-fifth published romance. In 1993 she won the *Romantic Times* Career Achievement Award for Best Storyteller of the Year, and her name was included in the list of winners sent to the White House by the American Booksellers Association. Cathie enjoys hearing from readers and has received fan mail from as far away as Nigeria!

An avid world traveler, Cathie often uses humorous mishaps from her own trips as inspiration for her stories. After traveling, Cathie is always glad to get back home to her two cats, her trusty word processor and her hidden cache of Oreo cookies!

This book is dedicated to
my editor, Anne Canadeo,
who has come full circle with me from my Dell
Candlelight Ecstasy days to this—my first special
project for Desire. They say fate works in mysterious
ways; I'm just glad its mysterious ways have reunited
us again! Thanks for going to bat for me. Thanks for
everything, including introducing me to my first Godiva
chocolates twelve years ago!

In addition, a special acknowledgment goes to
Nancy Colbert for getting me the inspirational
DDL poster!

One

"**I**'m telling you, the man was as naked as a jaybird!" Alberta Beasley declared in a loud voice.

Startled, Melissa Carlson looked up from the stack of books she was checking in at the circulation desk. Tiny Greely Public Library was normally deserted this early on a summer's morning. They'd certainly never had a problem with naked men before!

A split second later, Alberta's younger-by-three-minutes sister, Beatrice, said, "Nonsense. I've told you it's time to get your eyes checked again."

Melissa relaxed, realizing that the Beasley sisters, well into their seventies but as feisty as ever, were merely doing what they did best—bicker. For twins, they looked nothing alike. Alberta had short-cropped gray hair that reflected her steely personality. Beatrice was softer, her white hair gently curled and her twinkling blue eyes filled with compassion and gentleness. Alberta never *twinkled*. Her eyes were like steely lasers, missing nothing.

"What about you, Melissa?" Alberta asked the question, but both sisters turned to look at her expectantly. "Have you heard about our mystery man? The one who's naked as a jaybird up on the roof?"

"Are you telling me there's a naked man on the library roof?" Melissa asked in confusion.

"Not as far as I know," Alberta replied. "I'm talking about the naked man on the roof of the Poindexter cottage. Down by Moment Lake."

"And I say he wasn't naked at all but was wearing blue jeans," Beatrice inserted with a flutter of one of her ever-present lacy handkerchiefs.

"Either way, have you heard anything about him?" Alberta demanded of Melissa.

"No, I haven't." Call her selfish, but Melissa was infinitely relieved that something had happened in the normally quiet town to distract its residents from her own broken engagement to one of the town's most popular citizens. For the past week—ever since her fiancé, Wayne Turner, had taken off a mere ten days before their wedding—Melissa had been the unwanted center of attention in a town where ordinarily the only excitement this time of year came from watching the corn grow.

Melissa had heard the whispered conversations and the not-so-discreet discussions all about her being "dumped," about Wayne "flying the coop," about the short note her fiancé had left for her. Wayne hadn't even bothered to put the note under her *own* front door, Melissa noted bitterly. No, since the library was on the way to the interstate leading north to Chicago, that's where Wayne had left his written explanation before running off with Rosie from the Cut N' Curl beauty shop.

The news had gotten out fast, thanks to the fact that Wayne's curt note had been read by two other people at the library before Melissa had gotten her hands on it. In a small downstate Illinois town like Greely, where news traveled faster than a twister, the story of a broken engagement so close to the wedding date was cause for much speculation. The bad situation was made worse by the fact that Wayne had insisted on inviting almost the entire town to their now-canceled nuptials.

Not since Prince Charles and Diana had broken up had the women under the hair dryers at the Cut N' Curl had such a tantalizing bit of gossip to chew on. The men at the Weed N' Feed pretended that they were talking about the price of corn and soybeans, but Melissa had overheard enough to know better. Given the circumstances, Melissa was glad to have the glare of the town's spotlight moved onto someone else. The mystery man—whoever he might be—was on his own, poor soul.

"You mean we're the first to tell you about this mystery man? Good!" Alberta practically crowed with delight. "That means we've got a jump on that nosy Mrs. Cantrell."

Melissa had to smile at this blatant example of the pot calling the kettle black.

"I called the real-estate office and was told he's rented the cabin for a month," Alberta was saying confidingly. "They wouldn't tell me his name, though, just told me he's here on vacation. I ask you, who would want to come to Greely for a vacation? No one has rented that cabin in ages. The entire thing sounds suspicious to me."

Melissa knew from experience that *everything* sounded suspicious to Alberta Beasley, who imagined herself to be Agatha Christie's crime-solving Miss Marple incarnate. Alberta imagined everyone else, especially Mrs. Cantrell, as being just plain nosy.

As if on cue, Mrs. Cantrell came hurrying into the library, her face flushed with excitement. "Did you ladies hear about the mystery man—"

"Who has rented the Poindexter cottage," Alberta interrupted. "Of course we have. That's old news. We've even seen him. Have you? Did you get a good look at him?" Alberta demanded of Mrs. Cantrell.

"Well, I did see him on the cottage roof earlier," Mrs. Cantrell replied.

"Was he wearing clothes?" Alberta asked. "Or was he naked?"

"I'm not sure," Mrs. Cantrell said, clearly flustered.

"No powers of observation," Alberta muttered. "You're no help. We couldn't see him too well through the binoculars—"

"They're actually opera glasses and not meant for that kind of activity," Beatrice pointed out.

"We need one of those high-powered telescopes," Alberta maintained. "Anyway, all I could see was that he had dark hair and seemed good-looking. Also seemed to be buck naked. Maybe he's one of those nudists you hear about."

"He was wearing blue jeans, I'm sure of it," Beatrice maintained, daintily patting her forehead with her handkerchief. "Has he come into the library yet?" she asked Melissa.

"You think a nudist is going to use the library?" Alberta demanded in disbelief. "Sometimes you just don't make much sense, even though you are my sister."

"I'm telling you, he was wearing blue jeans while working on the roof," Beatrice reiterated. "The peak of the roof did keep getting in the way, but I could see that he has a very nice chest. Not so hairy that he'd look like a gorilla. Tanned and muscular.''

"Like the men on those romance novels you read." Alberta sniffed.

"That's right. The covers on *my* books are better than the covers on *yours,* all blood-soaked with guns and knives. But we're straying from the topic here. I wonder who this man is and why he's spending a month in Greely. Melissa, are you sure you don't know him?''

"What would make you think that *I'd* know him?'' Melissa asked.

"Because," Beatrice replied, "you're the only other person in town who has had anything exciting happen to them, other than the Olafsons having their cow birth twin calves.''

"You know, there was a full moon last night," Mrs. Cantrell pointed out. "People do crazy things around the time of a full moon. Crazy things like that nice fiancé of Melissa's running out on her." Mrs. Cantrell leaned over to pat Melissa's hand consolingly. "Who would have thought that such a nice young man, so popular in the community, would do something so wild? Practically leaving you at the altar. Why, we haven't had such a messy situation here in Greely since... Well, you know—" she gave Melissa a pitying look "—since that unfortunate incident with your mother.''

Melissa thought she'd prepared herself for the pain. She thought that she'd had her defenses well in place. But it only took a careless comment from Mrs. Cantrell for Melissa to realize how wrong she'd been.

"There wasn't a full moon when Wayne took off, so you can't use that excuse," Alberta stated bluntly. And then, to Melissa's relief, she said, "But let's get back to this mystery nudist.''

"You don't live far from the lake, Melissa," Beatrice pointed out. "Only two blocks away. As a neighborly gesture, you should go over and introduce yourself. Maybe he's single."

"And maybe he's an ax murderer," Alberta inserted. "Why are you trying to fix her up with a nudist ax murderer? Melissa's fiancé may have dumped her, but she's not that desperate yet. Right, Melissa?"

Melissa rubbed the spot between her eyebrows as she felt a major-size headache coming on. "I'm not desperate at all," she stated emphatically.

"See, I told you so," Alberta told her sister.

Melissa sighed and tried to hang on to what was left of her dignity. "If you ladies will excuse me, I need to get back to the books I was cataloging."

"Poor dear," Melissa overheard Mrs. Cantrell telling the others. "Can you imagine how humiliating it must be to come to work and find that your fiancé has left you and run off with another woman? I'd be mortified."

So was Melissa. For the first two days she'd been numb, as if the reality had been too painful to acknowledge. So she'd shut it off. But there was no way of avoiding the facts. There were plans that needed canceling—from the church to the flowers to the caterers—calls had to be made. And she'd made them, but with each one a little more of her had died as she'd tucked the ragged edges of her distress deep inside where no one could see.

"You can do this." Melissa's muttered pep talk was self-directed as she stood in front of the Poindexters' rented lake cottage, pie pan in hand. Unable to decide between the freshly baked strawberry-rhubarb and blueberry pies at Strohmson's Bakery in town, she'd gotten them both after work. It had only taken her half an hour to put away most of the first pie. Which was when she'd decided she'd better get rid of the second one before she ate it, too.

It was as much for her own protection as being neighborly, Melissa told herself. Since Wayne had left her, she'd already gained almost seven pounds. If she gained any more, the pink-and-white seersucker skirt she wore wouldn't fit, and it was a favorite of hers. Using her free hand, she nervously plucked at the collar of her white eyelet blouse while staring at the ladder leading up to the roof. While walking up to the rental cottage she'd checked the roof, but there didn't appear to be anyone working on it at the moment.

Aware of the bad luck she'd been experiencing lately and not wanting any more of it, Melissa deliberately made a point of not walking under the ladder—even though it blocked the entrance to the front porch. Instead she squeezed her way to the left of the wooden ladder, feeling the post of the wooden porch support biting into her back as she did so. The maneuver almost dumped the contents of her pie pan onto her shirtfront, but she prevented the blueberry disaster by righting the pan in the nick of time.

By the time she knocked on the front door, she was convinced this was a bad idea and therefore heaved a sigh of relief when no one answered. She quickly squeezed her way past the ladder again and was about to walk away when, out of the corner of her eye, she saw movement.

He was standing near the front corner of the house, holding a garden hose over his head to cool off. Beatrice was right. The mystery man was definitely wearing jeans, all right. And he had a *very* nice chest. A woman, any woman, no matter what her age, couldn't help noticing those two facts.

The water was running over his head, so she couldn't tell anything except that his hair was dark when wet. She followed the path of the water as it ran from his face and dripped onto his chest, where it trickled in rivulets over the tanned muscles to the waistband of his jeans, which rode low on his narrow hips.

He seemed to be deriving so much sensual pleasure from the play of the cool water over his clearly overheated body. Melissa was feeling rather overheated herself from just looking at him. She wasn't the type who normally ogled a man, but she couldn't seem to help herself in this instance. There was just *something* about him.

The material of his jeans was well-worn and hugged his body like a lover. She watched as a droplet of water rolled past his navel toward the snap of his jeans. And that's where she was looking when the man moved the hose away from his body and glared at her.

"What are you doing here?" he snapped.

"N-nothing," she stammered, hanging on to the pie pan for dear life. His eyes were green—vivid green—and they positively glittered with anger. At that moment it wasn't difficult to imagine that he *was* an ax murderer.

"Let me guess," he murmured mockingly. "You're the one they sent over to interrogate me, right?"

"What?"

"The pair of old biddies who have been spying on me all day."

"They aren't old biddies," Melissa protested on the Beasley sisters' behalf. "And they didn't send me over here."

"Then what are you doing here?"

"I was trying to be a good neighbor. Clearly the concept is beyond your comprehension," she retorted, angry enough to glare right back at him.

"I had no idea being a good neighbor included ogling in the description. Were you waiting for the rest of the show?"

"Listen, buster, you're not *that* good-looking, so don't kid yourself. I've seen lots better."

"I'll bet you have," he murmured.

Melissa was disconcerted by the predatory hunger she saw in his eyes. She hadn't meant that comment the way it sounded. "Coming here was clearly a mistake," she said. "I don't know what your problem is—"

"I'll tell you what my problem is," he shot back. "I came here for a little peace and quiet, not to be the center of attention from a bunch of sex-starved spinsters."

That did it! Without thinking, Melissa planted the blueberry pie smack in the middle of his chest.

His look of astonishment did her soul good. "Welcome to Greely!" she growled before pivoting and marching away.

Two

Oh my God, it was her! It wasn't until she'd thrown a fit and hit him in the chest with that pie that Nick Grant had realized she was Lissa—his protector from childhood days. Nick smiled ruefully. Lissa was still as fiery as she had been as a kid, fiercely coming to his defense when the other kids had picked on him.

Nick had been a sickly child—pale, thin and gangly—unable to keep up with the other children's active play, and therefore was frequently the butt of their jokes. A doctor had suggested sending him to the countryside instead of spending another summer in the city. So his parents, eager to transform their weakling of a son, had sent him to his aunt Faye in Greely. She'd been well into her seventies then and not much interested in keeping an eleven-year-old boy busy. But as a result of coming to Greely, he'd met Lissa—a terror of a tomboy with a right hook as good as any boy's in the neighborhood.

He remembered something had happened that summer…something to do with her mother…to make Lissa get a lot of practice with that right hook. The two of them had hung together as buddies against the rest of the world, even going so far as to become blood brothers, despite the fact that Lissa was a girl. She fought like a boy, and that was good enough for him. It had been her idea, of course, and the resultant cut on his thumb had ended up leaving a scar. But many a time he'd looked at that scar and gained strength from it.

Looking at it now, Nick shook his head in amazement, droplets of water showering his shoulders from his wet hair as he did so. Lissa. His protector. After all these years…

She hadn't recognized him. Granted, he hadn't recognized her, either, at first, but the minute she'd spit fire at him, he'd known it was her. It was too much for him to expect she'd remember him. No doubt that summer had meant more to him than it had to her. And he'd be the first to admit how much he'd changed…outwardly, anyway.

But still, Nick resented the fact that she hadn't recognized him. It wasn't logical, but then he never claimed to be logical. Which was why he found himself back in Greely after an absence of twenty-some years. He'd reached a crossroads in his life.

Midlife crisis at the age of thirty-three. His laugh held little humor, but then he'd had little to laugh about in life lately. Until a spitfire had dumped the pie on him, he noted with a genuine laugh this time. Using his index finger, he tasted the blueberry filling still clinging to his chest. Not bad.

Nick grinned as he recalled the belligerent way Lissa had stood—with her hands on her hips once she'd dumped the pie on him—just as she had as a child telling off the other kids for calling him names. But there was nothing childish about the curve of those hips. She'd grown into a woman. A woman he wanted to see again.

"So, my dear, did you get to meet our mystery man?" Beatrice Beasley called out as Melissa marched past her on the sidewalk. "Melissa, my dear!" Beatrice hurried after her. "I was speaking to you."

"What?" Melissa stopped as the sound of the younger Miss Beasley's voice finally sank in, interrupting her internal fury. "What did you say?"

"I asked if you met our mystery man," Beatrice repeated, dabbing at her face with an embroidered hankie.

"Yes, I did, and he's a jerk," Melissa stated succinctly.

"Was he wearing blue jeans or not?" Alberta demanded from beside her sister.

"He was definitely wearing jeans," Melissa replied, peeved with herself for remembering exactly how good he'd looked in those jeans.

"See, I told you so," Beatrice said to her sister with a nudge of her left elbow. "You owe me five dollars."

"Just because he's wearing jeans *now* doesn't mean he was before," Alberta shot back. "I don't suppose you asked him about that," the older woman turned to ask Melissa.

Caught up in her memories of lean hips encased in soft denim, Melissa shook her head as if to forcibly remove the stubborn image from her mind's eye.

"See, she didn't ask him," Alberta triumphantly informed her sister. "So I don't have to pay you five dollars. The bet is still up in the air."

So was Melissa's peace of mind. She hadn't felt this angry in years. In the moment she'd flung the pie at him, Greely's mystery man had represented *every* man—including the one who'd stood her up and left her to face the music.

Until this moment she hadn't allowed herself to feel angry at Wayne for his betrayal and desertion. She'd felt pain, humiliation, even guilt for not realizing something was wrong, for not seeing any sign. But this was the first time she'd experienced anger. And it felt good.

"My dear, are you all right?" Beatrice asked. "Your face is flushed, and you don't seem to be all here, if you don't mind my saying so."

"She's just got a lot on her mind," Alberta inserted. "Who wouldn't, in her situation?"

"I'm not in a *situation,*" Melissa stated with a direct stare in Alberta's direction, the first direct look she'd given anyone since she'd gotten Wayne's curt note. "And I don't appreciate you talking about me as if I weren't here."

"I don't like it when you do that, either," Beatrice confessed to her sister.

"You're just angry because you didn't win the bet," Alberta retorted. "And Melissa is angry because her fiancé was a weakling."

"Wayne wasn't a weakling," Melissa automatically protested, her spine stiffening. She'd always had a soft spot for defending those who were victims of name-calling. A vision flashed before her eyes of a pale, skinny boy wearing a pair of Coke-bottle-thick glasses. Nicky had been shorter than she was and not as strong physically. But that didn't mean he was a weakling. He'd had a purpose of mind and a determination she'd found impressive, even though she'd only been eight years old at the time.

In Wayne's case, he had a shelf full of trophies to prove his physical strength. He still held the county record for the most wrestling wins in one school year—a distinction he'd won in high school. And as coach, he'd taken the Greely Trojans to the quarterfinals in the state's football championship last year.

"It's good that you're angry with Wayne," Alberta was saying.

"I'm angry with just about everyone right now," Melissa muttered, rubbing her forehead and blowing her bangs out of her eyes. "Which means I'm not very good company. If you ladies will excuse me..."

"Of course, my dear," Beatrice said.

"She certainly didn't find out much," Alberta muttered.

"Hush, sister."

"I'll tell you this much," Melissa said. "Blue is *definitely* the man's best color."

With a grin, she left the Beasley sisters to their gossiping.

When Melissa went to work the next morning, she felt as if she'd lost some of the ground she'd gained last night. Her anger had sustained her until she'd gotten home. Then the empty house and the table filled with wedding presents still to be returned had gotten the better of her. Even the normally comforting presence of her long-haired calico cat, Magic, hadn't helped.

Heading for the freezer, Melissa had grabbed a pint of chocolate-chocolate-chip ice cream and dug right into it with her spoon, forgoing the use of a bowl. With one hand wrapped around the cold carton, she'd eaten most of it in one go—her hand going numb from the cold just as her heart felt numb and so very cold inside her breast.

Dreams lost. Trust betrayed. The tears had streaked her cheeks as she'd stood in front of the refrigerator with Magic forlornly meowing at her feet. The truth was finally sinking in. Melissa wasn't going to be wearing the gorgeous white wedding dress she'd picked out and had sent for all the way from Springfield. She wasn't going to be exchanging vows with the man she loved. She wouldn't be spending her life with him. It was all gone.

During her six-month engagement to Wayne, she'd finally started feeling as if she was part of the town's inner circle, as if her mother's scandal was no longer her own. Wayne's popularity in Greely had spread to her, and they'd attended parties, even joined the county's only country club. But those weren't the reasons she'd stood there crying last night. The bottom line was that the man she'd loved hadn't really loved her, after all. And that was the reason the tears had continued coming and hadn't stopped.

It was also the reason she'd been up most of the night, tossing and turning in her narrow twin bed to such an extent that Magic had jumped down in a huff and stalked off to sleep elsewhere. When Melissa finally had drifted off, it was to dream of a man with blueberry-pie filling trickling down his very muscular chest.

But now her dreams were finished and she had work to do, not to mention a curious public to face yet again. The traffic in the library had been heavier than usual for the past week, and Melissa knew the reason for that. The good people of Greely were coming into the library to see how "poor Melissa" was doing. She'd been "poor Melissa" when her mother had run away with the postmaster, leaving Melissa and her father behind. She'd been "poor Melissa" at sixteen when she'd been left behind as her father and his new wife and family had left for California. And now she was "poor Melissa" again.

Melissa refused to look the part. Eye drops had taken away the worst of the evidence from her crying jag last night, and while the chocolate-chocolate-chip ice cream hadn't solved her problems or alleviated her pain, it *had* made her feel better for a while. So had the memory of the mystery man's look of slack-jawed astonishment when she'd dumped that pie onto his bare chest.

Today she'd tried to lift her spirits by wearing a brightly colored floral dress to work. She'd taken special care with her makeup and hair. The end result was...okay. Melissa knew she'd never been a beauty. She had good bone structure, acceptable brown hair that curved into a smooth, shoulder-length cut, and good features. Feathery bangs hid most of her forehead, which she thought was too wide, anyway. She liked to think her blue eyes reflected her intelligence and that she was always ready with a smile. Wayne had told her she had a lovely smile. But then, Wayne had told her a lot of things.

Unfortunately, Melissa had finished the cataloging job that had kept her busy yesterday. The good news was that there seemed to be a momentary lull in the stream of people coming to the library to check up on her. For the first time in a week the place felt empty and deserted.

Melissa's footsteps echoed on the hardwood floor as she put away the newspapers that had been left strewn across the reading tables. Maybe it was time for her to look into getting another position, one in a larger town—a town that could afford to have a real budget and a real staff instead of a handful of volunteers on which Melissa had to rely. Maybe it was time for her to leave Greely.

But then her friend Patty Jensen arrived, reminding Melissa of why she'd stayed. Because of people like Patty. "So, how are you holding up?" Patty asked in that soft-spoken voice of hers as she joined Melissa at the reading table.

"As well as can be expected, I guess."

Patty gave her a hug. The two women had know each other since the sixth grade. Over the years, they'd shared confidences, laughter and tears. In a time of throwaway relationships, their decades-long friendship gave Melissa a stability that she valued more than she could say. Patty was to have been Melissa's bridesmaid at the wedding. She was also the first person Melissa had called after receiving Wayne's note.

"Is there anything I can do?" Patty asked now, as she had then.

Melissa shook her head. "You've been great, giving me moral support, keeping me sane."

"I wish there was more I could do." Patty suffered from a lifelong shyness, preferring to stay in the background in any situation. She'd been nervous about accepting the offer to be Melissa's bridesmaid, as she didn't feel comfortable with everyone's eyes on her. But she'd agreed to do it because Melissa had needed her. That's the kind of friend she was.

"Have the Beasley sisters been after you again?" Patty asked in a voice just short of a whisper. Alberta Beasley had intimidated her since Patty had been a child and Alberta had been the crabbiest kindergarten teacher imaginable.

"Not yet, but I'm sure they'll drop by later."

"I better get back to work," Patty said. She was a cashier at the Radizchek Drugstore, which sold everything from aspirin to zippers, and proudly announced that fact on their store window. "I'm just on my break. I'll touch base with you later."

After Patty was gone, the library was quiet once again. The thousand-square-foot building was a house that had been donated to the township to serve as a library. A contractor had donated his time to make some necessary modifications, and the library had opened its doors the summer Melissa's mother had left.

Little had changed since that time, in the library at least. Melissa had attempted to spruce things up, starting a monthly story hour for the toddlers, a reading club for the older children and a book sale to raise money for more acquisitions in the future.

The smaller of the two bedrooms had been converted into the reading room where she stood now. The room also housed the collection of reference materials and encyclopedias, as well as a pamphlet file. The other, much larger bedroom housed the nonfiction collection, while the fiction and new books of all kinds were shelved in the former living room. The brightly painted children's section was in the refurbished attached two-car garage.

Throughout the library, chairs were tucked into any available nook or cranny. There was also a study table near the circulation desk, which fronted what had at one time been a galley-style kitchen and was now Melissa's work area. There wasn't an inch of wasted space and certainly no room to spare.

The library was open forty hours a week, closed Sundays and Mondays. Melissa had planned on taking her two-week vacation, during which time the library would have been closed, as her honeymoon. When the wedding was canceled, she'd canceled her vacation, as well, promising herself a short trip later in the summer—one she'd have time to plan on her own.

She hadn't a clue where Wayne had planned on taking her for their honeymoon. He'd insisted she leave all the plans to him, and so she had. Those days were gone.

Later that afternoon Melissa was sitting at her desk, composing letters to various agricultural agencies requesting free material for the pamphlet file, when she got the feeling that someone was watching her. Looking up, she saw Greely's mystery man standing at the circulation counter. He was wearing a plain white T-shirt and was carrying a cardboard box. He was also looking at her expectantly.

Melissa had had to deal with troublemakers in her library before—from twelve-year-old Dennis, who tried to sneak a smoke in the washroom, to ninety-year-old Mr.

Obersdorf's insistence that the library carry *Playboy*. She could handle this mystery man, too—whoever he was.

"I brought you something," he said.

She didn't bite, instead letting a long silence fill the air.

"After your quaint welcoming ceremony yesterday, I thought the least I could do was return the favor." Seeing her tense up, he said, "Relax. I'm not going to throw it at you." He opened up the carton to show her the pie inside. "It's blueberry. To replace the one that got ruined last night."

"You didn't need to do that," she said, still cautiously keeping her distance.

Nick felt a stab of disappointment. Even this close up, without him being sopping wet, she didn't recognize him. He'd held out the hope that she would. That her face would light up, and she'd smile at him. No such luck. His disappointment was followed by anger—at himself and at her for making him have such foolish thoughts.

"Why, hello, Melissa, I hope I'm not interrupting," Mrs. Cantrell said as she entered the library. Coming closer, she hovered nearby, eyeing Nick with undisguised curiosity. "So, you two know each other, hmm?"

"No," said Melissa.

"Yes," said Nick simultaneously.

"You're not interrupting anything, Mrs. Cantrell," Melissa firmly stated. "What can I do for you?"

"I was wondering if that Dean Koontz book had come in yet?" Mrs. Cantrell asked Melissa, while keeping her eyes on the man beside her.

"No," Melissa replied. "As I told you yesterday, it will probably take another week to ten days before it will be back. You're next on the waiting list."

"Oh, that's right." Mrs. Cantrell fluttered her lashes at Nick while speaking to Melissa. "You did tell me that. I must have forgotten in the excitement of all the goings-on around here lately." Finally turning her gaze to Melissa, she said, "So tell me, are you feeling better, dear? I still can't believe that dear Wayne would do something like this." The implication being that Melissa must have done something to make a good man like Wayne dump her at the last minute. "Have you heard anything more from him?"

"No, and I don't expect to," Melissa said stiffly.

Mrs. Cantrell made a sympathetic clucking noise. "That's such a shame. You seemed like the perfect couple. Well, I suppose I'd better go and leave you two to whatever you were doing." She hurried out, clearly eager to spread the news of the mystery man bringing Melissa goodies from Strohmson's Bakery.

Melissa closed her eyes at the image of Mrs. Cantrell blowing the incident completely out of proportion. It would be all over town in fifteen minutes.

"Who's dear Wayne and what did he do?" Nick demanded with a dark intensity that made her eyes fly open again.

"That's none of your business," Melissa retorted.

"I'm making it my business."

"Who do you think you are?" she shot back.

"*I* know who I am," he replied, "but you don't, do you?"

"Is that your way of implying that you're someone important? Because if so, I'm not impressed."

"You looked impressed last night," he dryly pointed out.

Melissa glared at him.

Nick smiled. "You know, the last time I saw you lose your temper, you split Biff's lip wide open for blackening my eye. Remember that, Lissa?"

Three

Oh, my God, it was *him!* It was her childhood buddy, Nicky—trapped in the body of a hunk. Talk about the Twilight Zone! Melissa could hardly believe her eyes. But it was *his* eyes she focused on.

As if mentally asking, *Are you in there?* she moved closer to stare directly into his green eyes. It was him, all right. The cocky grin had thrown her at first. So had his powerful presence. But it was his eyes she remembered from their childhood—eyes that had been much too old for an eleven-year-old boy.

He'd grown up...and how! That summer so long ago he'd sported a crew cut. She remembered how the other kids had mercilessly teased him about that, since longer hair had been the fashion. Now his black hair was thick and long, almost brushing his shoulders at the sides while a few much shorter locks fell recklessly over his high, distinguished forehead.

Far from being straight or the least bit stringy, his dark hair held a rebellious wave that defied taming.

The gangly, awkward boy he'd been was only distantly echoed in the angular cheekbones, the square jaw, the lean build. Her gaze shifted from his face to his shoulders beneath the white T-shirt, and she was struck by the confidence of his posture. The Nicky she'd known had perennially been bent over in a slouch, as if trying to remain invisible.

Of course, that had been over twenty years ago. A lot had happened in that time. Not the least of which was the transformation Nick Grant had gone through, as if he'd been honed by fire.

"Cat got your tongue?" he inquired dryly, meeting her stunned gaze head-on.

"You look—" she waved her hand in his direction "—different."

"So do you. I didn't recognize you until you plastered that pie in my chest."

Melissa blushed at the memory of how she'd lost her temper. "I'm sorry about that—"

"Don't be," he interrupted. "I deserved it. The Lissa I knew would have hit me with more than a pie."

"The Lissa you knew is gone," she quietly told him.

"I don't think so." Leaning closer, he studied her as thoroughly as she'd studied him a moment ago. "She's in there someplace. I just wonder what happened to make her so subdued."

"Life happened."

"Life with 'dear Wayne'? What did the jerk do to you?"

Melissa paused, unwilling to admit that Wayne had dumped her. But Nick would be hearing about it sooner or later. At the moment, she preferred it to be later, however.

Changing the subject, she asked, "What are you doing back in Greely after all this time?"

"I'm here on vacation," Nick replied.

"This isn't exactly the vacation capital of the world," she pointed out.

"I came for some peace and quiet. I had some thinking to do."

"Peace and quiet. Sounds nice." Melissa longed for a little of that herself.

"Look, if it makes you feel any better, I've heard some talk about your wedding being called off."

"Then why did you ask who Wayne is?" she demanded, feeling uncomfortable again.

"I wanted *you* to tell me about it. There was a time when we shared our problems."

"That was light-years ago."

"I've got a good shoulder to cry on," Nick said.

She'd noticed that. A good shoulder to go with that great chest of his.

"Come on," he coaxed. "You always used to say I was a good listener."

"Why are you so interested?" she countered.

"Because you were a good friend to me once, and I'd like to repay the favor. Seems to me you could use a good friend right now."

He was right about that, she had to admit. Patty had done her best to be supportive, but Melissa didn't like to dump too much on her friend, knowing how sensitive she was.

"How about we talk over dinner tonight?" Nick suggested. Seeing her hesitation, he added, "What better distraction for the local gossips than for you to be seen with the town's mystery man? That would give them something to talk about, rather than whispering about poor Melissa. It would show them you're getting on with your life, instead of hiding yourself away in the library mooning over your ex-fiancé.''

Angered by his words, Melissa said, ''I'm not in hiding and I'm not mooning. You don't know what it feels like to be jilted the way I was!''

''I certainly *do* know about humiliation, Lissa. In fact, I'm an expert, having had years of experience with it while growing up.''

''That was different,'' she muttered.

''How so? Being publicly rejected and ridiculed results in the same kind of pain you're feeling right now. Which is why I'm determined to help you the way you helped me when we were kids.''

''There's no need—''

''Yes, there is. So let's give this town something else to talk about. What do you say?''

Melissa didn't know what to say. She still wasn't used to the fact that this lean, dark hunk was her childhood buddy. ''I need some time to think about it.''

''Fine. Think about it all you want. But like it or not, I'm going to help you.''

His attitude infuriated her. ''How like a man to think he always knows what's right.''

''That's better,'' Nick noted approvingly. ''I prefer the light of battle in your eyes to the panicked look of a trapped bird.''

''I don't care what you prefer,'' Melissa shot back.

''Not yet, but you will.'' Seeing the telltale fire in her eyes, Nick grinned and took a step back, out of pie-throwing range. ''Ah, there she is—my Lissa is back! I hope she sticks around. Could make things *very* interesting.'' Whistling softly, he moseyed on out of the library.

Melissa barely had time to stash the blueberry pie out of sight under the counter before the Beasley sisters breezed in.

Alberta was looking over her shoulder. "I'm telling you, Beatrice, there's something about that man.... I'm sure I've seen him before."

"Of course you've seen him before," Beatrice concurred. "Through the opera glasses. Yesterday."

"No, I mean I've seen him before that. Did you check those posters in the post office? The ones of the wanted criminals?"

Beatrice nodded.

"And?" Alberta prompted.

"And nothing. He didn't look like any of them."

"All right, Melissa," Alberta stated as she turned her attention away from her sister. "This is a job for you, with your reference skills. My sister and I have already done some preliminary checking. She checked the wanted posters, I checked my video tapes of *America's Most Wanted* shows last night. Can't place him yet, but we will. I never forget a face, and I'm sure I've seen that man before. Mrs. Cantrell told us she saw you and the mystery man chatting like old friends. Claimed he came courting you with bakery goods." Alberta sniffed as if she found that hard to believe. "Now, I realize Mrs. Cantrell can be a busybody and she elaborates her stories, but I thought I'd better check this out with you."

"Check what out?" Melissa inquired, deliberately playing dumb. She wasn't in the mood to be accommodating at the moment.

"The mystery man, of course. I know you're pining away for Wayne, my dear, but you really must try and concentrate. Did the man speak to you, Melissa? We know he was here, because we saw him leaving as we came in."

"Yes, he spoke to me."

"And? What did he say? Did you get any information out of him? Come along, Melissa, don't be shy. Speak up."

Beatrice spoke before Melissa could. "You're being bossy again," she chastised her sister, with a flutter of her lacy handkerchief. "Don't be impatient. Melissa will tell us in her own time, won't you, dear?"

"I'll bet he threatened her and that's why she's so quiet," Alberta declared.

Knowing how vivid Alberta's imagination was, Melissa decided it was time to come clean with the truth before they dreamed up some wild scenario. "The reason he looks so familiar is because he's been to Greely before."

"I knew it!" Alberta said triumphantly. "I knew I'd seen him before."

"Who is he?" Beatrice asked.

"Nick Grant," Melissa replied. At their blank looks, she added, "Mrs. Abinworth's nephew, Nicky. He spent the summer with her when he was eleven."

"I distinctly remember that Mrs. Abinworth's nephew was as scrawny as a scarecrow," Alberta stated.

"He grew up," Melissa said.

"I'll say!" Beatrice murmured.

"I don't believe it," Alberta stubbornly maintained. "There's no way he could change that much. He told you he was Mrs. Abinworth's nephew, did he?"

"No, he didn't tell me. I recognized him myself."

"You didn't recognize him when you went over to his cottage yesterday," Alberta pointed out.

"As you said, he's changed."

"Changed too much to be true, if you ask me," Alberta stated. "Did you ask to see some ID? A driver's license or something?"

"Of course not."

"Why not? I thought prospective library patrons had to show some ID if they wanted to use the library."

"Only if they want to get a library card. And he didn't come here to get a library card."

"What did he come here for?"

"To apologize for being curt when I visited him yesterday."

"What was his excuse?"

"He didn't recognize me, either. Not until I . . ." Melissa broke off, not in any hurry to confess to hitting Nick with a pie.

"Not until you what?" Alberta demanded.

"Got angry with him," Melissa substituted.

"Why did you get angry—" This time it was Alberta who broke off as a new thought occurred to her. "The man wasn't naked when you went visiting yesterday, was he? I distinctly recall asking you about that at the time, and you assured us that he was definitely wearing pants. You weren't fibbing to protect our sensibilities, were you, dear?"

"Of course not. He just wasn't very friendly, and I got angry with his arrogant attitude. So he dropped by the library today to apologize, and that's about it."

Alberta frowned suspiciously. "Sounds like there's more you're not telling us. What about the box from Strohmson's Bakery that Mrs. Cantrell said she saw on the counter? Was he trying to butter you up with sweets?"

"With *his* looks, he doesn't need to butter a woman up," Beatrice dreamily inserted. "He could pose for one of my romance covers!"

"He has the chest for it," Alberta grudgingly agreed.

"Speaking of romances, we got in that hardcover book you were waiting for, Beatrice," Melissa stated, eager to get off the topic of Nick Grant.

The sisters left a short while later, clearly irked that Melissa wasn't willing to disclose more than she had. Melissa also had a sneaking suspicion that Alberta wasn't buying the fact that Nick was who he said he was.

Melissa had *no* doubts herself. Although Nick had changed in many ways, the similarities were still there to those with the sensitivity to see beyond his Black Irish good looks to the man inside.

As Melissa sat at her desk, her gaze kept wandering to the pie Nick had brought her. She'd have to give it back to him. She didn't need another pie around her place. She didn't need any additional temptation. She was trying to be good— to be stoic—when the truth was she felt as mixed up as raw dough. She'd take the pie back tonight, as soon as the library closed at seven.

That evening, Melissa retraced her steps to Nick's rented cottage, wondering why he'd returned to Greely. It was hardly the typical place for a vacation. He'd said he wanted peace and quiet. They *did* have plenty of that. The small town had almost eighteen hundred inhabitants and was surrounded by flat farmland. Moment Lake was one of several in the area that provided a nice break from the acres and acres of planted fields. Within Greely itself, tree-shaded streets were laid out in meticulous precision. But not meticulous enough to have made Nick return.

Melissa lived near the northern edge of town, so it was only a two-block walk to the lake. Actually, the blocks gave out before she got to the lake and turned into wooded area that used to have a few cabins. The Poindexters' was the only one left standing. The others had fallen into disrepair. Too many families leaving Greely for greener pastures.

Melissa had stopped at her place long enough to change out of her work clothes into a more comfortable outfit of electric blue tank top and black cotton walking shorts. Her white gym shoes were scuffed from frequent wear over the years. She supposed it was time to buy a new pair, but she'd spent most of her available clothing funds on a honeymoon trousseau. Gym shoes hadn't been on the list.

She supposed she should take back some of the clothes that still had the store labels on them, maybe get a refund or a credit to buy something more practical than lace-trimmed silk nighties and strapless sundresses.

Wayne had hinted that he'd be taking her someplace warm for their honeymoon. He'd said he wanted to surprise her. He certainly had.

Not for the first time, Melissa wondered if there had been signs that he'd been about to be unfaithful to her. Signs that she, in her blind happiness, hadn't noticed. She'd mentally gone over their last days together, searching for some clue to where she'd gone wrong. Knowing now what she didn't know then, *every* word he'd said sounded suspicious, so clearly she wasn't yet in a position to judge things objectively.

When she reached the cabin, Nick was once again standing with a garden hose in his hand. Only this time, he had it aimed at his car and not at himself.

"You're busy," she noted, telling herself she was relieved because that meant she didn't have to stay. "I just came by to return this pie to you. I don't need it. That is, I brought the pie yesterday for you, so since this one replaces it, it's for you, as well." Cursing her stumbling tongue, Melissa snapped her mouth shut, her face turning red.

"It's time for me to take a break, anyway," Nick said, setting down the hose and turning off the water at the side of the cabin. "What're you drinking? Iced tea or beer?"

"No, really, I can't stay...."

But he was already gone, leaving her standing there with the pie still in hand.

"I brought you a beer," Nick said a minute later, letting the screened porch door slam shut behind him. "Seems to me you could probably use one after the day you've had."

"What do you know about the day I've had?"

"I saw those two remnants from the Spanish Inquisition entering the library as I left it today. They looked ready to give you the third degree."

Melissa shrugged. "They were curious about you."

"I gathered that from their surveillance of me with the binoculars the other day," he noted dryly.

"How did you know they were using binoculars? Actually, I think they were only opera glasses, and they couldn't get a very good look, but still . . ."

"I saw the sun flashing off the glass through the trees." Nick sat down on one of the director's chairs on the front porch and patted the other one invitingly. "Come on, set yourself down and take a load off."

"Which is another reason I'm returning the pie to you," Melissa said. "I don't need to gain any more weight."

"You look fine to me," Nick noted with an approving head-to-toe look in her direction.

"Thank you, but you don't have to be kind. I know I've filled out."

"In all the right places," he added with a grin that flashed like sunlight off the lake.

"Yeah, right," she said, climbing the steps to the porch and sitting in the chair beside him. She set the pie on the small table nearby and took the cool beer can he offered her.

"I can get a glass for that if you'd rather."

"No, that's okay," she said, struggling to open the can without breaking a fingernail. She'd already broken two nails this week and bitten off three others. She wanted to protect the few she had left.

Nick solved the problem by taking the can and flipping it open for her.

"Thanks," she murmured.

"No problem."

They sat there in silence for some time, which surprised Melissa. She'd forgotten how comforting his presence could be. When they were kids, they'd been able to just sit and enjoy one another's company for hours on end. They'd also talked up a storm when the occasion warranted it. The neat thing was that she'd felt comfortable with him either way—in silence or in a rush of conversation.

"This is nice," Nick murmured.

Melissa wasn't sure if he was referring to the coolness of the breeze off the lake, the bubbly frothiness of the beer or her company. Perhaps even a combination of all three. But she agreed, it *was* nice.

"I remember sitting like this when we were kids," Nick reminisced. "Course, we were drinking root beer in those days. And you were always barefoot. Couldn't keep a pair of shoes on to save your life."

Melissa smiled. "I'd forgotten that."

"You mean you got over your barefoot days? That's a shame. You had cute feet. And you used to wiggle your toes when you were happy."

"You've got an incredible memory."

"Only when things are important to me."

Turning his head, he stared at her in a way that had a disturbing effect on her metabolism. Unnerved, she quickly looked away.

"You're welcome to kick off your shoes if you want to," he invited her. "Here, I'll join you." He kicked off his athletic shoes and propped his bare feet on the porch railing, handily nearby.

An instant later, Melissa had her shoes off and her feet propped next to his. Ah, heaven. She wiggled her toes.

Looking his way, she shared a grin with him.

"Feels good, huh?" he noted teasingly.

She nodded. "I'd forgotten how good."

"So had I," he said.

They shared the silence again. Actually, it wasn't completely quiet, as the early evening air was filled with the sounds of nature—the somnolent hissing of cicadas, the sharp call of a cardinal to its mate. The air was filled with the scent of honeysuckle, which grew in profusion alongside the porch and up the slightly crooked white trellis.

The peaceful interlude was brought to an end when Melissa shifted her foot on the railing and ended up with a splinter in her heel. An ouch had escaped her lips before she was able to stop it.

"What did you do?" Nick demanded.

"I got a splinter in my foot," she noted in disgust.

"Here, let me look." He waylaid her foot before she got it to her own lap and placed it, instead, on his thigh. Leaning over, he examined her heel. "Yep, there's a splinter, all right. A big one, too." His fingers cradled her foot as he held it up to get a better view.

His touch communicated both his strength and his tenderness. The contact was nerve-tingling, generating a singing current from her foot up her leg to places beyond. Flustered, Melissa stared at his hands with their long, lean fingers gently moving over the paleness of her skin. His nails were cut short, and he had the wide finger span of a pianist or an artist. He was certainly creating havoc within her as she became acutely aware of his slightest move.

"Hold still," he ordered as she wiggled in her seat. "Okay, I see it now." He pulled the splinter out. "There." He tossed the wooden fragment over the railing. Squeezing her foot, he made sure that the flow of blood cleansed the wound. "Stay put, I'll go get a Band-Aid for you."

He was back a minute later.

"Now I remember why I stopped going barefoot," she muttered. "It's all coming back to me." Grimacing, she placed the adhesive bandage on her heel before putting her shoes on. "Well, I should be going, anyway."

"Did you give any more thought to my plan?" Nick said.

"Yes, and I don't think it would work. No one is going to believe that you're interested in me as anything other than a friend."

He frowned at her, making his wide brows look even darker. "Why not?"

"Because a man like you wouldn't ordinarily look twice at a woman like me."

"What the hell is that supposed to mean? I'm a man like any other man."

"A better-looking one than most," she inserted.

"Who grew up being a *worse*-looking one than most," he reminded her. "Trust me, I know how it feels to be judged by my cover, whether it be good or bad."

"I'm sorry."

"You should be," he shot back. "I expected better of you."

"So shoot me," she retorted. "I'm human."

"And humans have failings, huh? I'm glad you realize that. This afternoon you were trying so hard to be the perfect little librarian."

"First off, I'm not little," Melissa angrily declared. "As I recall, I was taller than you were when we were kids, and while you might have sprouted up in the last twenty years, I'm still no shrimp. Secondly, don't say librarian like that—as if it's an insult. Librarians are just like anyone else. We're nothing like our stereotypical spinster image. So I'm not married. So what? I'm good at my job. I'm not a withered-up old prune!'' she practically shouted.

"I never said you were," he said quietly, his tone conveying the message that he understood more than he was saying.

Melissa whispered, "The woman my fiancé ran away with was barely twenty-one, did you know that?"

Nick shook his head.

"A *gorgeous* twenty-one-year-old."

"How old is Wayne?"

"Thirty-nine."

"Old enough to know better," Nick declared.

"Don't tell me that you wouldn't run away with a beautiful young thing if you got the chance," she scoffed.

"I've had the chance," Nick said bluntly. "And I didn't take it."

"So you're a saint. Most men aren't."

"Since when have you become an expert on men?" he inquired dryly. "I'm willing to bet that Wayne was the first serious man in your life."

"Well, you'd bet wrong."

"Okay, so he was the second."

Melissa shoved her bangs out of her eyes, remembering how she'd disliked it when he'd matter-of-factly pointed something out when they were kids—usually something she didn't want to hear. "How did we get started on this subject, anyway? How come you don't talk about *your* love life?"

"Maybe because I don't have one."

"I find that hard to believe," she inserted.

"At the moment," he continued with a slow smile.

"And have there been a lot of women in your life?" Seeing his frown, she said, "Hey, what's good for the goose is good for the gander. You've asked me intimate questions, it's only fair that I return the favor."

"I'll admit that when I was in my early twenties, and women finally started noticing me, I ate up the newfound attention. It was heady stuff at first. But it got stale pretty quickly."

"Oh? Why's that?"

Nick shrugged. "I'm not cut out to be some woman's pretty boy."

"There hasn't been anyone serious?"

"There was one. We broke up last year. Actually, she dumped me. So I *do* know how it feels."

"Are you over her?"

"Is that your way of asking if you ever get over it?" he astutely inquired. "If so, the answer is yes."

"Did you love her a lot?" she asked wistfully.

"I didn't love her at all."

"But you said it was serious."

"It was."

"I don't understand."

"No, you wouldn't."

"If you didn't love her, then you can't know how it feels to have the person you love jilt you," Melissa maintained.

"Do you still love Wayne?" Nick demanded.

She nodded slowly.

Nick looked at her in amazement.

"It's not an emotion you can turn off with the flick of a switch," Melissa said defensively. "Listen, I've got to go."

"You need me more than I thought," Nick murmured.

"I don't *need* you at all."

"Okay, fine. But I need that garden hose at your feet," he said as he followed her from the porch and headed toward his car. "Hand it to me for a second, would you?"

She did, and he used it to quickly wet the surface of his white Volvo before handing it back to her. "Thanks."

Her fingers brushed his, instigating another rush of confusing excitement. As if burned, Melissa dropped the hose onto the ground—whereupon the nozzle trigger activated and, with a spurt, sprayed water right in her face.

Nick laughed at her stunned expression. "You should see yourself!"

His laughter broke the tension created by their earlier serious discussion. Leaning down to grab the now quiet garden hose, Melissa said, "So you think that was funny, do you? Then watch this." She aimed the spray directly at him. "Maybe I should have said *wash* this," she noted with a grin as Nick sputtered.

Seeing him sopping wet reminded her of their encounter the day before, when she'd watched the water run over the lean, tanned muscles of his bare chest to the waistband of his jeans. At the moment his white T-shirt was sticking to him like a second skin.

"You little devil!"

"I told you not to call me little," she reminded him with an arch smile and another spurt from the spray nozzle.

"Give me that," he ordered, leaning across the hood of the car to try to grab it from her. He won the ensuing tussle, although he got doused again in the process. So did she. Once he had the hose in his possession, Melissa quickly backed away.

"Now, Nick, enough's enough. Let's quit and call it even."

"No way!"

"You never used to hold a grudge," she reminded him.

"I don't hold a grudge. I get even." Snaring her in one arm, he said, "Gotcha!"

Melissa squeezed her eyes shut, expecting him to thoroughly soak her with water. Instead she heard him drop the hose and felt his lips brushing hers. "Don't look now, but the old biddies are spying on us," he whispered against her mouth. "Let's give them something to look at, shall we?" Without waiting a second longer, he settled his lips on hers.

Four

—

Nick's lips were warm on hers, startling her with their enticing persuasion. For a man who was supposedly just putting on a show, he was doing a darn good job of it, Melissa dizzily noted. Where had he learned to kiss like this? There was no hint of the awkwardness or shyness that had plagued him as a youth.

Nick's movements were sure and confident as he gathered her even closer. Confused by the sensual pleasure sweeping through her, Melissa gave no thought to protesting. His kiss was evoking a reckless excitement that was both awesome and fascinating. Her heart was pounding as he explored the curve of her lips with the velvety tip of his tongue. He was tantalizing her, inviting her tongue to join his in play. Ultimately, it was an invitation too good to refuse.

Hesitantly, Melissa parted her lips, allowing him entrance. She half expected him to storm the pearly gates of her teeth, but he didn't. Instead, Nick seemed to be satisfied with dallying at the threshold as he used his tongue to slowly taste the inner curve of her bottom lip before sampling the outer corner of her mouth. She needed no further convincing as she blindly responded to the promise of sensual delight he was offering.

Their kiss deepened, becoming a mutual exploration that progressed beyond excitement to fierce hunger. Entwining his fingers in her hair, Nick gently shifted her head just a smidgen so that her mouth angled against his with even greater intimacy.

Moving with subtle expertise, he drew her to him by small increments until their bodies were as closely aligned as their mouths. Widening his stance, he pressed her to him tightly. Cradling the back of her head with the palm of his hand, he continued tunneling his fingers through the silky strands of her hair. His other hand rested on the small of her back, his splayed fingers causing licks of fire to dance down her spine.

In the nether regions of her mind, Melissa vaguely thought she heard the sound of her name followed by someone clearing his or her throat. It couldn't be Nick. He had no breath left to clear his throat. Neither did she. She didn't seem to care. Breathing seemed highly overrated at the moment and couldn't compete with the irresistibly compelling need to continue their kiss.

She heard her name again, this time spoken with an authority guaranteed to cut through the deepest sensual haze.

"Melissa!"

As if jabbed with a cattle prod, Melissa jerked out of Nick's arms.

"Excuse us for interrupting, but we thought you'd want to hear the news," Alberta stated crisply as she and her sister stood nearby.

"News?" Melissa dazedly held her right hand to her lips, which were still throbbing as a result of Nick's kiss. It was a pleasurable rather than a painful feeling. "What news? Is something wrong?"

"Depends what you mean by wrong," Alberta replied with a shrug. "Wayne is back in town. And Rosie's not with him."

Melissa was still dazed from Nick's kiss, so the Beasley sisters' news was slow to sink in. "Wayne..."

"That's right. Your fiancé," Alberta said.

"*Ex*-fiancé," Beatrice and Nick corrected in unison.

"Wayne's back?" Melissa repeated, finally snapping to attention.

"And he doesn't have Rosie with him," Beatrice repeated.

Wisely or not, hope flared within Melissa. Maybe Wayne had come to his senses. Maybe he'd realized it had been a mistake to leave her.

Nick read the look of hope on Melissa's face as clearly as if it were written in neon lights. Surely she couldn't still have feelings for a guy who was such a jerk as to leave her practically at the altar? Okay, so not five minutes ago she'd admitted she still loved Wayne, but Nick hadn't given much credence to her confession. Not after what the guy had done to her. The Lissa he knew would never have stood for such treatment. She'd have blackened the eye of anyone who tried to treat her like a fool. But she was also incredibly loyal, he reminded himself. She'd never been one to change alliances easily or quickly.

"We thought you'd want to hear right away, Melissa," Alberta said with a disapproving look in Nick's direction.

"Thank you," Melissa said. "I'd better get going." She hurried down the gravel drive as if pursued by ghosts.

Nick moved to follow her, but was stopped by the united front of the Beasley sisters.

"So you say you're Nick Grant?" Alberta made the statement sound like a question.

"That's right."

"And your aunt's name was..."

Amused by their blatant curiosity, Nick decided to play along. "Faye," he replied laconically.

"Her last name, I meant," Alberta clarified.

"Abinworth."

"And she was born when?"

"In June sometime."

"That's not very specific," Alberta commented. "June of what year?"

Nick shrugged. "I never asked her. We weren't that close."

"That I can believe," Alberta said, making it clear she believed little else.

"You ladies have a problem?" Nick inquired.

"No, of course not."

"We just don't want to see Melissa hurt," Beatrice inserted.

"Neither do I," Nick stated. "If you recall, the two of us were close as kids."

"The two of you were *close* not five minutes ago!" Alberta muttered.

"Until you interrupted us," Nick replied.

Alberta drew herself to her full height and stared down her nose at him, no easy feat since he was nearly six inches taller than she. Her voice was chilly as she stated, "We thought Melissa should know that Wayne is back."

"Actually, I thought we should wait to tell her," Beatrice timidly tacked on.

"You clearly are the more sensitive sister," Nick noted, taking Beatrice's hand and bowing over it as if he were a courtier of old.

"Oh, my," Beatrice said with a fluttery smile and a wave of her lacy handkerchief.

"Come along, sister," Alberta snapped. "It's time we were leaving!"

Melissa closed the front door behind her with a breathless gasp. She had a stitch in her side from rushing all the way home. She'd made it. She was safe. For the time being.

Making her way into the living room, she sank onto the plush couch that Wayne had thought uncomfortable and Melissa had always loved. She curled up on its down pillows and leaned her cheek against the damask apricot material on the back.

It was her favorite thinking pose, and goodness knew she had tons of thinking to do. So much so that she couldn't even decide which to think about first—Nick's unexpected kiss and her even more unexpected reaction to it, or Wayne's return.

Wayne. Of course, she should think about Wayne first. He was the man she loved, the man she'd planned on spending the rest of her life with.

Nick was... She wasn't ready to think about Nick yet.

Wayne. Why had he come back to town without Rosie? Could it be that he'd made a mistake and had come back to make things right? Could they even be made right?

Melissa rubbed her forehead, making her bangs stand out like silky spikes in the process. A second later she got a face full of long-haired fur as her cat, Magic, walked along the back of the couch much like a tightrope walker in a circus.

"So, Magic, guess who's back in town? Wayne."

At the sound of his name, the cat held up her nose disdainfully before sitting down.

"Yeah, he's back. Without Rosie. Do you believe it?"

Magic paused in the process of washing herself to scratch her ear, thereby shaking her head.

"Yeah, I know." Sighing, Melissa rubbed Magic's ears. "We were supposed to be married this weekend, you know."

The cat closed her eyes and purred in ecstasy.

"What a life," Melissa murmured. "You've got it good, don't you? Just remember one thing, don't ever fall in love. It's the pits."

Magic purred, butting her head against Melissa's hand.

When the phone rang, Melissa ignored it, preferring to let her answering machine screen her calls as she'd done since Wayne had left. But when she heard who was calling, she leaned over and grabbed the receiver. "Hi, Dad! It's me. I'm here."

"This is just a quick call," her father stated.

Melissa silently noted that *all* of his infrequent calls were quick. He'd also been quick to remarry after Melissa's mother had run away with the local postmaster. And Melissa's new stepmother, Vivien, had been equally quick to make her opinion known loud and clear—that Melissa was a burden rather than a stepdaughter, an outsider rather than a family member. Vivien never even bothered to hide her preference for her own two daughters. Her father had never stood up for Melissa in the past.

"I'm calling about the bread maker," her father said.

They'd sent her a bread maker as a wedding present. "I received it, thanks," Melissa replied. "I sent you a note, didn't I?"

"Yes. But, well, the thing is, given the fact that your wedding is off and all . . . We just thought that since you're not going to use the wedding present, you might want to return it. You know, your stepsister has always wanted one. And with her and David just moving into their new home..."

"I'll return it to you tomorrow," Melissa said, barely able to get the words past a throat that had gone taut with tension.

"Fine," her father said in a jovial tone. "I'll call her and tell her it's coming. 'Bye now."

He never even asked how I was doing, Melissa realized as she shakily hung up. Granted, he'd never been the most sensitive of fathers, but even so, she'd thought that given the situation he'd at least ask how she was holding up.

She needed to learn to stop expecting anything. Then she wouldn't be disappointed. After all, her days of believing that a man would be her champion were long gone, disappearing along with all the other mementos of her childhood that her stepmother had thrown out before they'd sold the house and moved to California.

Only sixteen at the time, Melissa had chosen to stay behind in Greely to finish high school rather than pull up roots. She'd never been accepted by her father's new family, anyway. But like a kid pressing her nose against a candy-store window, there was still a part of her wishing she could be on the inside, wishing she could be part of a real family.

The phone rang again. This time it was Patty. Needing to talk to a friend, Melissa picked up.

"I called a minute ago, but your line was busy," Patty said.

"My father just called."

"What did he want? I'm sure he wasn't checking to see if you're all right," Patty noted, having seen firsthand during their younger years how badly Melissa had been treated.

"He wants me to return the wedding present they sent me," Melissa replied thickly. "Seems my stepsister has always wanted a bread maker."

"Of all the nerve!" Patty's normally mild voice seethed with indignation. "I'd have told him where he could put his bread maker!"

"No, you wouldn't have. And neither did I. I told him I'd return it tomorrow. I'm not going to keep something he'd rather give to my stepsister." The same way he'd preferred giving his time and his love to her stepsisters, and never to her.

"Your dad always did have rotten timing," Patty noted. "I don't want to make you feel even worse, but have you heard the news about Wayne?"

"That he's back in town? Yes, I heard."

"And Rosie isn't with him."

"I heard that, too."

"What are you going to do?" Patty asked.

Melissa laughed unsteadily. "I don't know. Burn him at the stake?"

"Sounds like a plan to me," Patty concurred vehemently. "I'll even light the matches for you."

"If only it were that easy," Melissa said, her laugh sounding perilously like a sob.

"You still love him, don't you?" Patty said, her soft voice filled with empathy.

"Yes." Melissa wiped the tears away as quickly as they fell.

"Oh, Melissa . . ." Patty sighed.

"My sentiments exactly." It would have been simpler had her love for Wayne died the moment she'd gotten his curt note. But it hadn't, and she had to live with that fact.

* * *

Another mostly sleepless night brought Melissa into the library the next morning with extreme reluctance. She'd been so tempted to call in sick this morning. But there was no one to cover for her today.

As it was, her first patron of the day was none other than Wayne Turner, her ex-fiancé. His light brown hair was cut short, shorter than when he'd left. His usually gleaming blue eyes were strangely cautious, and they matched the color of his polo shirt—the one with the Lincoln High School insignia on it.

She looked at him in dismay. She wasn't ready for this meeting yet.

"We need to talk," Wayne said.

Her heart skipped a beat. "Have you come to tell me that you made a mistake?" she asked.

Wayne shook his head. "I came because this is a small town and sooner or later we're bound to bump into each other."

"Bump into her and you'll bump into me," Nick stated from the library doorway, having just entered the small building. "And I don't *like* being bumped into. In fact, I'm downright sensitive about it."

Melissa had thought the situation couldn't get any worse than it already was, but Nick's unexpected appearance made her revise that idea.

"And you are…" Wayne inquired with a frown in Nick's direction.

"Melissa's protector," Nick proudly proclaimed as he came closer with the unhurried movement of a man who knew exactly where he was going. "Who are you?"

"Wayne Turner."

Nick nodded. "Oh, right. The jerk."

His face flushed with anger, Wayne turned to confront Melissa. "Who is that guy, Melissa?"

"Nick Grant. Mrs. Abinworth's nephew."

"Or so he says," Alberta Beasley piped up from the background.

Where had *she* come from? Melissa felt like pounding her head on the circulation desk. Instead she politely inquired of Alberta, "Is there something I can help you with?"

"No, I was just browsing. Looking for a good book. Don't mind me." She looked at Wayne as if just noticing him for the first time. "Why, Wayne, what a surprise to see you here."

"I live here," he replied. "Of course I'd be back."

"I meant here at the library," Alberta said with a meaningful look in Melissa's direction. "And how is Rosie doing? Is she with you?"

"No. She's still up in Chicago, finishing a two-week seminar on beauty makeovers."

"Oh, so that's why she's not here with you."

"That's right."

"So... nothing has changed between you two? You and Rosie, I mean."

"Nothing has changed," Wayne said, clearly looking uncomfortable with this line of conversation.

"Of course things *have* changed here," Alberta continued. "Nick Grant is the new mystery man in town. He and Melissa used to be... close."

Wayne didn't look very pleased at the idea.

"Melissa and Mrs. Abinworth's nephew were playmates as children," Alberta elaborated.

"I don't recall a Nick Grant growing up in these parts," Wayne noted with a disapproving look in Nick's direction.

"He only visited with his aunt for one summer," Melissa inserted when Nick made no move to respond to Wayne's unspoken question.

"Doesn't the man speak for himself?" Wayne inquired mockingly.

"Only when it's important," Nick laconically replied.

"Well, Nick," Wayne said in a hearty man-to-man voice that never failed to work with the kids on his football team. "I'd like to have a word in private with Melissa, if you don't mind."

"I *do* mind," Nick stated.

"No, he doesn't," Melissa inserted, her eyes pleading with him not to cause a scene.

Nick's steely expression slowly changed to one of impatient resignation before he turned, irritation clearly vibrating in his movement and posture. "I'll be right over there if you need me," he said, indicating the magazine rack on the other side of the room—out of earshot but close enough to see trouble coming.

With Wayne and Melissa both staring at her, Alberta had the good grace to give in, as well. "I'll go over there with him, just to make sure he doesn't steal any of those magazines," Alberta muttered before trailing after Nick.

"This isn't the place for a private conversation," Melissa informed Wayne once they were alone, or as alone as they were going to get. "I'm working now."

"I just wanted to drop by and let you know I was back in town rather than having you hear about it from someone else."

"It's too late for that. Surely you know how fast this town's gossip mill is? No, perhaps you don't—since you left before the fat hit the fire," she noted angrily. "Well, let me be the first to tell you that every detail of our broken engagement has been grist for the gossip mill during the past week."

"I'm sorry about that, Mel," Wayne said, using his nickname for her. "I never meant to hurt you."

"Then why did you?" she asked unsteadily.

"I couldn't marry you when I had feelings for Rosie. Surely you can understand that," he said with a pleading look. "It wouldn't be right."

She steeled herself not to give in. "Oh, and I suppose it was right to take off ten days before the wedding, just leaving a note for me here at work? A note that anyone could read—and did?"

He had the grace to look contrite. "Okay, so I'm guilty of bad timing."

"Why did you ask me to marry you in the first place, Wayne?"

"Because I loved you. You know that."

"And you stopped loving me?"

"No. That's not it. Feeling the way I did, I mean the way I *do* about Rosie, it wouldn't have been fair to you for me to go ahead and marry you."

"Didn't it ever occur to you that I deserved to be told face-to-face?" she demanded, unable to hide the betrayal she'd felt.

"Yes. You did deserve that. I'm sorry I couldn't do it. I couldn't bear to see that look of pain on your face. So I took the coward's way out, I admit it. But I'm back to face the music now."

His words struck her like knives. "Is that what I am? The music? Your punishment?"

"Mel, I didn't mean that the way it sounded...." Wayne's voice trailed off, regretful. But it was the look in his eyes that did her in, for it was a look of pity.

The idea of Wayne feeling sorry for her, of *him* viewing her as "poor Melissa," was more than she could bear. "I think you'd better leave now," Melissa said in a strangled voice.

"I want us still to be friends," Wayne pleaded.

Too upset to speak, Melissa shook her head. She didn't breathe until Wayne left, and then it was to inhale with the unsteadiness of one gasping for air.

"Are you all right?" Nick appeared at her side to softly ask her.

Melissa bit her lip to stop it from trembling. "I'll be fine," she lied. "I just want to be left alone."

To her relief, Nick didn't press her. Instead, he came to her rescue by taking Alberta Beasley with him. "This would be the perfect time for the two of us to sit down over at the Dairy Queen and chat about my aunt Faye," Nick informed a startled Alberta. "Feel free to ask any questions you like."

It was an invitation Melissa knew Alberta wouldn't be able to refuse. As the two left together, it occurred to Melissa that Nick had a way of issuing invitations too good to refuse. For the moment, thinking about Nick was easier than thinking about Wayne and the crowning humiliation of having him look at her with pity instead of love.

Melissa had just finished eating dinner, a veritable feast of junk food including cheese balls and black olives, when there was a knock at her front door. She was tempted to ignore it. She wasn't in the mood for company. Since leaving work she'd been trying to hold back the depression threatening to completely inundate her, but it was like trying to hold back the night.

Opening the door, she found Nick on the other side of the screened storm door. Once again he was holding a familiar-looking box from Strohmson's Bakery in his hands.

"I have a problem," he declared with an overly dramatic sigh.

"You do?"

Nick nodded. "This blueberry pie is just too good to eat alone. Something this good has to be shared."

"You're right," she said before unlatching the screen door and inviting him inside.

"I'm right?"

"The notion surprises you?"

"No. The notion of you agreeing with me is what surprises me. Or maybe I should say that the notion of you *admitting* you agree with me is surprising."

"Stop while you're ahead," she advised him with a wry smile. She took the box out of his hands and set it on the coffee table. "Come on in and sit down while I go get something to cut this with and some plates. Would you like something to drink?"

"Do you have any milk?"

She nodded, her smile turning into a full-fledged grin as she recalled their milk-drinking contests as kids, vying for who had the widest milk mustache. Next to root beer, it had been their favorite drink. "You still drink the white stuff?" she inquired teasingly.

"Only on special occasions," he said with equal humor.

It occurred to her that Nick would make a good ad for the American Dairy Council—good, strong bones and good teeth—were it not for the fact that his features were too rugged to be considered wholesome. There was too much character etched on his forceful face, and there were too many mysteries in his green eyes. Too much knowledge in his slow smile. No, Nick wasn't a wholesome, ruddy-cheeked farm boy. He was a dangerous, granite-cheeked man, too good-looking for a woman's peace of mind.

When she returned from the kitchen, she found him sitting in the armchair rather than on the couch. She was pleased by his choice, because it meant that she could sit on the couch and have some space. He wasn't crowding her. The distance between them made it easier for her to cut the pie with efficiency and hand it to him on a plate without betraying any of her nervousness.

"I confess I had an ulterior motive in dropping by tonight," Nick said.

Instead of rising to the bait, Melissa ate her pie and waited for him to continue in his own sweet time.

"I thought it would be a good time to have a strategy meeting," he elaborated, before taking a sip of the cold milk.

Melissa watched the white liquid touching his lips, watched the way his Adam's apple moved as he swallowed. There was no milk mustache this time. His upper lip was thin and somewhat aesthetic, while in contrast his lower lip was full and sensual.

As her gaze shifted up toward his eyes, she belatedly realized he was frowning at her as if expecting her to speak. She frantically dug back in her mind to remember what he'd just said. "Strategy meeting?"

Nick nodded. "About the best way of dealing with your situation."

"Moving to Antarctica sounds appealing about now," she replied.

"I don't think you need do anything quite that drastic," he wryly responded. "Although I admit that I did wonder over the years if you'd stayed here or moved elsewhere."

"I went to college in Chicago, but never felt as if I fit in. I wasn't happy in such a big city. In fact, I was miserable. So

I went to Urbana to get my master's degree and then I came back here and ended up renting this house. In a small town like Greely, the unfortunate fact is that there are more people moving *out* than moving in. The owners of this house had been looking for someone to rent it for some time.''

''It's a beautiful old house,'' Nick noted admiringly. ''A good example of Victorian Gothic, a master carpenter's romantic vision of a medieval cathedral translated into wood.'' His quiet voice was filled with reverence. ''They don't build them like this anymore—steep gables and pointed arch windows are the Gothic elements, while the projecting bay window and etched glass are classic elements of Victorian architecture. You've also got some fine detailing on the door canopy and bargeboard. No, they sure don't build them like this anymore.''

''You sound like an expert. And what's a bargeboard?''

''A bargeboard is the board hanging from the projecting end of a sloping roof,'' he replied.

''You mean that white lacy board attached to the roof? I just call it gingerbread trim.''

''Made possible by the introduction of the steam-powered scroll saw,'' he told her, ''so that carpenters could cut elaborate designs much more quickly and economically than by hand.''

''Yep, you definitely sound like an expert,'' she noted.

''I'm an architect,'' he said.

''Really? That's great! You always did like building things,'' she recalled. ''Remember that fort we made down by the lake? The one in the big willow tree? It had two levels.''

''And a great view,'' he added.

''Right into the window of Peggy Sue Hammond's upstairs bedroom, as I recall,'' Melissa said with a grin. ''And you have the nerve to accuse the Beasley sisters of snooping."

"Takes one to know one," he countered with a slow smile. "Besides, the sight of Peggy Sue in her black bra was too good to pass up. Whatever happened to her?"

"She has five kids and recently got divorced, so she may be available if you're still interested."

"No, thanks."

As they continued reminiscing about the days gone by, Melissa began to relax and feel at peace for the first time... for the first time since they'd sat on his front porch yesterday. Once again, his company comforted her.

His company must also have reassured her cat, because Magic came out of hiding and displayed her curiosity about this newcomer in her territory by jumping on the arm of his chair. Rather than being irritated by the cat's boldness, as Wayne so often was, Nick spoke softly to the cat and won her undying devotion by scratching the long-haired feline in her favorite spot—directly behind her left ear.

Magic's purr was loud enough to hear clear across the street.

"Your cat likes blueberries," Nick noted as the cat licked some of the syrupy fruit from his fingertip.

"She's nearsighted," Melissa replied. "She probably thought you had something really good, although she does have a sweet tooth."

"How can you tell when a cat's nearsighted?"

"There are several signs. For one thing, she puts her nose on yours in order to get a good look at you, just like she's doing now," Melissa noted with a grin. "And she misjudges distances, which means she sometimes misses what she's aiming at. Because of that, the animal shelter couldn't find anyone else to take her, so I did."

As the cat jumped down, he quietly asked, "Still trying to take care of the underdog or the *cat* as the case may be, Lissa?"

"What are you talking about?"

"I'm talking about the way you always champion those in need. The same way you tried to take care of me when we were kids."

"You make it sound like a wretched trait."

"Only when you fail to look out for yourself first. Is that what attracted you to Mr. Football Coach? Was he another case for you to take care of?"

"How can you say that? Wayne is a very confident and very successful coach. What makes you think he'd need taking care of?"

"The fact that he's weak." When she would have protested, Nick held up his hand. "I'm talking about morally weak, Lissa. Look at the facts. The jerk left you and ran off with a woman almost half his age. That's the sign of a man who doesn't know who he is, who's feeling threatened by his age. A man who's insecure."

"Oh? And I suppose *you've* never been insecure?"

"You know better. Of course I have. But I never cheated on a woman to make me feel like more of a man." After having met Wayne at the library that afternoon, Nick couldn't understand how his brave Lissa could have fallen for a dumb jock like that. Nick knew the type. He'd met plenty of guys like Wayne over the years. Their neck size was bigger than their IQ. They were the ones who, until he'd reached his twenties, had taken delight in torturing him for his lack of brawn and his abundance of brains.

To Nick's way of thinking, Wayne represented all the thickheaded lug heads in the world. Personally, Nick preferred other ways to show his strength rather than hammering someone on the five-yard line. It only went to show him yet again how far Melissa had moved from her true self. The self he was determined to return to her.

"So back to our strategy plan," Nick said. "The object here is to stop people from calling you poor Melissa. Agreed?"

Melissa nodded, shoving her bangs out of her eyes as she did so. "Agreed."

"Good."

"Now what exactly does your plan entail?" she wanted to know.

"Since when has the fearless Lissa started looking before she leaps?" Nick countered.

"Since her fiancé dumped her," she retorted.

Privately, Nick thought it had been much longer than that. Aloud, he said, "Didn't you look before leaping with him?"

Yes, she had. A lot. For all the good it had done her. The rotten thing was that despite everything, she wasn't over loving Wayne. But seeing that look of regret and pity he'd given her at the library had firmed her resolve never to see that look in anyone's eyes again.

"Point taken," she noted.

"So are we partners?"

She nodded and held out her hand, thumb held up for the special handshake they'd shared so many times as kids. His hand engulfed hers as she huskily said the words that went with their handshake. "We are friends . . ."

"Till the end," Nick completed, sealing their age-old vow with a look that had nothing to do with childhood and everything to do with passion.

Five

Melissa awoke Sunday morning to the sound of hailstones hitting her bedroom window. Groaning, she tugged the pillow over her head. She hadn't gotten to sleep until almost three. She planned on sleeping through this day—pretending it never happened, skipping right over it—and the fact that it was to have been her wedding day.

The shower of hailstones continued, this batch sounding like they were the size of baseballs. For safety's sake, she decided she'd better take a quick look out the window and make sure a tornado wasn't about to descend on her. Shoving the pillow away, she got out of bed and squinted against the slice of bright sunshine peaking through her drapes.

Since when had hailstones been accompanied by sunshine? Pulling aside the drapes, she looked outside. The sky was blue. Lowering her gaze, she saw Nick standing in her backyard, leaning down to pick up another handful of gravel from her drive. His pose gave her a good look at his backside, encased in jeans that fit like a glove and clung to his long legs as he bent over. Today his T-shirt was blue. He looked too good for words.

She opened the half-sash windows and stuck her head out. "What do you think you're doing?"

"Getting your attention."

"What for?"

"Let me in, and I'll tell you."

"I'm not in the mood for company," she told him.

"I'm not company," he replied. "You know, I'm sure I saw Mrs. Cantrell walking her dog across the street a few minutes ago. If you'd rather she didn't overhear us, you'd better let me in."

Muttering under her breath, Melissa grabbed a cotton robe and stomped downstairs. Nick was waiting for her on the back porch.

"I brought you something," he told her, holding up a bag from Strohmson's Bakery before unpacking it to hand her a paper cup of black coffee and a Danish.

"You're trying to make me fat," she accused him even as she took a bite of the Danish.

"Hey, if you don't want it..."

She slapped his hand away. "Never come between a woman and her Danish first thing in the morning," she warned him before adding a belated, "thanks for bringing this over."

"I figured you could use some sustenance. We've got a busy day ahead of us."

"This is news to me."

"It's meant to be. So go get dressed and we'll get started."

"Started doing what?"

"Enacting our master plan."

She shook her head. "Not today."

"Most certainly today."

"I'm not in the mood."

"Poooor Melissa," he crooned mockingly.

Just as he'd hoped, her eyes shot fire at him.

"That's better," he said approvingly. "And while you look quite fetching in that nightshirt, I don't think it's appropriate for a day at the lake. Wear something . . . skimpy. Got any halter tops? Or better yet, a bikini top."

"Since when have you become a fashion consultant, Nick?"

"Since I agreed to help you."

"It wasn't *my* idea that you help me," she reminded him, her pride stung a bit by his claim.

"No, it was much too good an idea to have come from you," he willingly agreed.

"I've had plenty of good ideas," she retorted. "Agreeing to go along with this plan may not have been one of them, however."

"Too late for cold feet now," Nick informed her, before adding, "it's going to be a scorcher today. The less you wear, the better."

Melissa gave him a narrow-eyed look over the rim of her cup of coffee. It was only then that she noticed the half-moon-shaped thin cut near his left eye, which lent him a piratical look.

"What did you do to yourself?" she demanded, abandoning her Danish to get a closer look at his injury.

"Would you believe I was in a duel to defend your honor?"

She gave him a skeptical look.

"Okay," he confessed. "I ran into a tree. Well, not exactly ran into it. I was out running in the woods on the south side of the lake and I didn't see this branch until it hit me in the face. Got my attention then, I can tell you."

"You're lucky you didn't poke your eye out," she scolded as she gently grasped his chin in her fingers and turned his face toward the sunlight streaming through the kitchen window. Shaking her head, she added, "You need to watch where you're going. You always were blind as a bat. Which reminds me, whatever happened to the glasses you used to wear?"

"I traded them in for contacts."

"Which could have made hitting your eye even more dangerous. You really need to be more careful when you run."

He lifted her hand and pressed it against his cheek. "Yes, ma'am."

Feeling the sharp angle of his high cheekbone beneath her fingertips, Melissa was unable to resist slowly tracing her index finger from the cut near his eye...down his cheek...to the square lines of his jaw. The raspiness of a day's growth of beard on his face made her skin tingle from the friction.

Their eyes caught. His look was the same one he'd given her when they'd sealed their pact with their secret hand-shake two days ago. The flare of passion was powerful in its intensity.

What was she getting herself into here? Melissa wondered in dismay, tearing her eyes away from the magnetic hold of Nick's gaze. She dropped her fingers, nervously grasping them with her other hand as if to forcibly prevent them from returning to his face.

She loved Wayne, she reminded herself. Nick was just being a friend. Helping her out in a tough situation. She must have misread his expression. Lack of sleep could do that. Make a person's thinking muddled.

Melissa's fingers were still tingling, the feel of his skin seemingly forever etched in her sensual memory banks. Quickly excusing herself, she hurried upstairs to change.

"Remember, think skimpy," Nick called after her.

She could tell by his tone of voice that he didn't really think she'd take him up on his instructions.

Well, she was about to show Nick Grant and the rest of Greely that they didn't know her as well as they thought they did! Poor Melissa, the jilted bride, was replaced by Warrior Woman Lissa and she dressed accordingly.

The cutoff jeans were just barely this side of decent, while the bikini halter top she wore made the most of her thirty-four C bra size. To make matters worse, she added a very sheer cotton poet-style blouse that displayed every inch of bare skin beneath it. The effect was more tantalizing than if she'd worn the bikini top alone. She'd ordered the outfit from a lingerie catalog for her trousseau. Instead, she was using it as battle gear.

It worked. She saw the way Nick's jaw dropped when he caught sight of her. In fact, he almost choked on the rest of her Danish, which he was finishing up.

Patting him on the back, she made commiserating noises. "Is this skimpy enough?" she inquired innocently.

"You get any skimpier, and I'll have a heart attack," he gasped.

"Well, we wouldn't want that now, would we."

"That's some blouse you're wearing," he noted with a shake of his head.

"I thought so, too."

"Not something from poor Melissa's wardrobe."

"You've got that right."

"Wayne is an incredibly stupid jerk to have let you get away," Nick said in that quiet but commanding way of his.

Melissa had to blink quickly to hold back the tears. "Thanks," she whispered. "You're a real pal."

"Yeah," Nick muttered as he followed her out of the house. "That's me, all right. A real pal."

* * *

"Are you paying attention?" Nick asked as Melissa stretched out next to him on a blanket spread next to the lake.

"Mmm."

"I'm going to read you some excerpts from this book I got for you. It's called *Mating Rituals*. I thought the chapter most applicable in this case would be 'How to Get the Man You Want—How Bodies Attract.'"

"You're making this up," she said without so much as cracking an eye open.

"I am not. Look for yourself." He waved the book under her nose. The sunglasses she wore prevented him from seeing her expression, although he did note the beginning of a frown on her forehead. "Are you sure you put enough sunscreen on?"

"I'm sure. Stop worrying."

"I'd feel better if I'd applied it myself. I'm not sure you could see what you were doing."

"I could see just fine," she lazily assured him.

"Then maybe you should put some more sunscreen on me. I think I'm burning here," he muttered with a dark look in her direction. She'd abandoned her sheer blouse altogether, and while she'd kept her cutoffs on, all they did was make him wonder if she was wearing the matching bikini bottom under them.

"I just put sunscreen on you not fifteen minutes ago, Nick. It couldn't have worn off yet." Melissa knew that the effect of touching him with the slippery coconut-scented cream certainly hadn't worn off yet. Her heart was only now starting to settle back into anything resembling a normal rate.

"Aren't you hot lying there like that?"

"Mmm," she murmured agreeably.

"Maybe we should sit on the dock and catch some of the lake breeze. You know, dangle our feet in the water and cool down."

"I'm too comfortable to move."

Nick muttered something under his breath that she couldn't quite hear. "What was that?"

"I said that according to this book, confident behavior will magnify the image others have of you." To himself, Nick added the postscript that certain parts of his anatomy were becoming almost painfully magnified as a result of Melissa's sexy attire. "It also talks about chests." His eyes rested on *her* chest, the tanned swell of her breasts clearly evident beyond the material of her halter top. He wondered what she'd say if she knew that he was dying to have her in his arms, to lower his mouth to those luscious curves and see if they tasted as sweet as they looked. To glide his tongue over the firm peaks, to cup her in the palm of his hand, to take her into his mouth even as he came into her....

"Do go on," she requested.

Feeling his tongue sticking to the roof of his mouth, Nick had to clear his throat before being able to continue. "Uh, it says that a man's chest is in close competition with his shoulders for basic 'huggability' where women are concerned."

Resting her eyes on him beneath the protection of her sunglasses, Melissa had to agree. Nick had discarded his T-shirt and was just wearing jeans. It really was a crime to cover up a chest like his, she decided, while being very much aware that she wasn't the only woman in Greely to feel that way. But she was the only one to see beyond that—to know something of the man inside. He had a rare kind of honor—the kind that chivalrous knights of old had. The kind that meant he'd walk through fire for someone he loved.

Nick wouldn't be an easy man to love. He didn't share himself easily—unlike Wayne, who was always able to socialize with ease, who made strangers feel as if they'd known him for years. But with Nick, the closeness would be all the more valuable for its rarity. The woman who loved him would be privy to a part of him no one else was.

But that woman wasn't her. It couldn't be her. She wasn't looking for more complications in her life. How could she be having these feelings for Nick when she'd been engaged to Wayne a mere ten days ago? Today she was to have married Wayne. She still loved him. Didn't she? Of course, she did. She'd never been the kind of person to change her feelings overnight.

"It says here that women prefer men who are barrel chested." Nick frowned, remembering Wayne's stocky build. "It also says they aren't to be trusted," he fabricated. "That skinny guys are the best."

"I don't know any skinny guys," she replied.

"You know me."

"You're tall and lean, not skinny. Not anymore. But you already know that. I'll bet a million other women have already told you."

"I don't care about a million other women. I care about you."

"I know you do." She sat up and slid her sunglasses so that they perched atop her head. "And I appreciate your friendship, honestly I do. Who'd have thought that after all these years you'd ride into town on your white horse to save me."

"I came in a white Volvo. And I'm not the knight in shining armor type."

"Sure you are."

"I didn't know you were in trouble when I came here. I just wanted to get some thinking done."

"And instead, you found yourself saddled with me. It's not fair of me to be taking so much of your time when you came down here with your own agenda." She stood up as if to leave, but Nick reached out to tug her down again, perilously close to him this time.

"I came here to think about my future. I'd like to talk about it with you," he said.

"I'd like that," she murmured.

"You already know that I'm an architect. In Chicago. For one of the largest architectural firms in the city. What you don't know is that I'm not happy doing it any longer."

"Why not?"

"It's hard to put into words. I've been a workaholic for so long. Nose to the grindstone." He picked up her hand, the one that had been nervously shredding the blades of grass next to his thigh, and he spread her fingers out over his bent knee—carefully arranging each one equidistant from the next. "I took this month's leave because I hadn't taken any time off in over five years. The vacation days were piling up, and personnel wasn't happy with the way they were accruing."

"What made you come back here? You could have gone anywhere...."

Staring out over the lake, he continued absently playing with her fingers before slowly replying, "I spent some of the happiest days of my life here. With you."

"But that was a long time ago."

"I have a long memory," he said almost pensively.

"So do I." The connection his touch was creating was something she'd have a very hard time forgetting. Yet she didn't pull her hand away. She couldn't. And she didn't want to. It felt too good, too right, to be forming this bridge with him. "So tell me why you aren't happy at your job in Chicago."

"Because I'm no longer doing the things that made me want to become an architect in the first place. My time is spent designing yet another strip mall, yet another corporate office complex. Ripping up more and more fertile farmland to pave it over with cement. Did you know that two million acres of farmland in this country are lost to development every year? That's five thousand acres a day! And I'm ashamed to have been contributing to the problem instead of doing something to help solve it. And then there are the historical buildings we're knocking down...." Nick shook his head. "Don't get me started," he muttered.

"You said you're not doing the things that made you want to be an architect. What were those things?"

"The idea of creating something. Of seeing your vision come to life. Of valuing the simple beauty in the horizontal lines of a prairie school building. Or the elaborate detailing of a château-style mansion. Appreciating the diversity of design. I've made a very good living the past ten years, but now I seem to have reached a midlife crisis."

"You're a little young for that, I think," she noted with a smile. "I think you're evaluating what you want out of life. And that takes courage."

He shrugged off her words. "It's easy to be courageous when you've got a safety net. I've got money stashed. If I were really courageous, I'd have left when I first became dissatisfied with what I was doing and I'd have struck out on my own then. Hell, I should have struck out on my own to begin with."

"To leave a sure thing for uncertainty always takes courage, regardless of when you decide to do it."

He turned his attention from the lake to her, studying her with the same single-minded stillness. "How'd you get to be so smart?"

"I had an eleven-year-old boy teach me a lot about inner courage and strength."

"You were the one who always stood up for me, not the other way around."

"As I recall, you were always there to support me when I'd come crying on your shoulder about something someone had said about my mother," she noted.

"And you'd decked them with that lethal right hook of yours. But you never talked much about what set you off."

"That was the summer she left and created such a scandal in town. She ran off with the postmaster, leaving her family behind. Everyone was talking about it. They still do, sometimes. Especially now that her daughter has a scandal of her own to contend with."

"A scandal not of your own making."

Feeling a sudden chill, Melissa freed her fingers from his loose hold and reached for her blouse. "I don't want to talk about it today."

"Okay." To her relief he didn't push it. "What do you say we take a little boat trip around the lake?"

"Who's got a boat?"

"I do. Came with the cabin rental."

Fifteen minutes later they were out on the lake. As Melissa trailed her fingers in the cool water, it was easy to imagine that they were miles away from Greely. The straw hat she'd brought in her tote bag made her feel like a Victorian lady being wooed by her beau as he rowed her up the Thames.

You've been watching too much "Masterpiece Theatre," she chastised herself. And Nick wasn't her beau, although he was handsome enough to make any Victorian lady swoon. Especially now, shirtless, muscles rippling as he smoothly dipped the oars into the water. The sunlight glinted off his dark hair.

Noticing her attention, he muttered, "I've got to get this cut." Since his hands were occupied with the oars, he couldn't brush away a strand that was coming close to falling into his eyes.

So Melissa leaned forward and gently brushed it away for him, her fingertips tracing the outward curve of broad eyebrows as she did so. Surely it couldn't be a good sign that she got such pleasure out of touching him. The sound of a thunderclap seemed to be a judgmental rendering from above and she guiltily leapt in her seat.

On the western horizon a storm was rapidly approaching, its blue-black color signaling its fierceness.

Swearing under his breath, Nick quickly turned the rowboat and headed toward shore. A lake was not a safe place to be in an electrical storm. As if to reinforce that realization, lightning zigzagged from the sky.

The heavens opened when they were still fifty yards from the dock. By the time they secured the boat, they were both soaked to the skin and shivering—the temperature had dropped twenty degrees in as many minutes.

Grabbing her hand, Nick raced toward the cabin. Once inside, he flicked on the light switch near the door to dispel the gloom, but nothing happened. "The electricity must have gone out."

"It happens with s-storms as b-bad as this one," Melissa noted through chattering teeth.

"You're soaking wet."

"So are you."

He steered her toward the small bathroom. "Get out of those wet clothes and into a hot shower. I'll start a fire out here. Did you bring any dry clothes with you?"

She nodded, pointing to her tote bag, which they'd left at the cabin when they'd decided to head out in the boat. "B-but I'll need a new shirt," she said.

"Fine. I'll get you one." Shoving back the shower curtain, he turned on the hot water. "Hurry up and get in while the hot water holds out."

A second later he was gone, closing the door behind him.

Melissa's fingers shook as she hurriedly undid her cutoffs. It never ceased to amaze her how quickly the weather could change. One minute it could be sunny, the next storming. Her arms got tangled in her sheer blouse as she tried to peel it off. Her underwear and halter top followed and then she was standing beneath the heavenly flow of warm water. Remembering what Nick had said about there not being much of a supply, she didn't waste it but only used enough to get warmed up.

She'd just turned off the faucet when she heard the sound of the bathroom door opening. "I brought you a shirt," Nick said. "I'll leave it hanging from the doorknob."

Peeking around the edge of the shower curtain, she made sure the bathroom door was closed again—with him on the other side of said door—before she hopped out the shower and quickly wrapped a bath towel around herself. He'd also hung her tote bag from the doorknob. Digging inside it, she pulled out the colorful broomstick-pleated cotton skirt she'd brought along, in case they opted to stop somewhere to eat. She'd also packed a silky purple camisole, which could have been worn under her sheer poet blouse, had it been dry. As it was, she put on just the camisole.

Since her bikini underwear was still soaking wet, she opted not to put it on until it was a little drier. The shirt he'd gotten her was a white cotton one and big on her. She rolled up the sleeves several times and tied the excess material from the shirttails into a knot at her waist. He'd also added a pair of white athletic socks, which she put on.

Looking into the steamy mirror, she decided she looked like some pirate's wench with her long skirt and man's shirt.

Her wet hair was wrapped in a white towel, and her bangs
curled in damp tendrils across her forehead. The makeup
she'd applied had long since washed off, and she'd only
brought lipstick with her—so that was the only thing she
could apply, which she did.

Leaving the bathroom, she found that Nick had indeed
got a fire started in the natural stone fireplace that took up
a good portion of one wall. A few colorful throw pillows
from the couch had been set out near the fire in an inviting
position. He'd changed out of his wet jeans into a dry pair
and had tugged on a new T-shirt. This one was white.

"The electricity is still out," he told her.

"Do you have a portable radio handy?" she asked as she
removed the towel to rub her hair dry. "Maybe we should
turn it on to see if there are any weather warnings out."

"Good idea." He turned on the old-fashioned clock radio on top of the equally old-fashioned fridge, both of
which had probably been around since Eisenhower was
president.

They found a weather report on one of the golden-oldies
stations. "Thunderstorms will be moving through the area,
but the weather bureau hasn't issued any watches yet," the
report claimed. "Stay tuned right here for any changes in
that situation. Meanwhile, here's a classic by Boz Skaggs.
It's 'Lido.'"

The sound of superior rock-and-roll sprang from the radio's tinny speaker. Grinning, Nick turned the volume
louder before holding out his hand to her in an invitation to
dance.

Dropping the towel she held, she joined him. It wasn't a
tune you danced cheek-to-cheek to. It was one you let slide
down your spine and set your feet moving, matching the
rhythm of the bass. The fact that they were both wearing

socks made their feet move all that much easier over the slippery surface of the wooden floor.

Nick moved with the same supple male grace he displayed when walking. He wasn't excessive in his actions. He didn't have to be. She grinned her approval as she circled him, swaying to the music, creating her own movements as she went along. Her full skirt swirled around her legs as she played off Nick. Melissa had never felt so free, so gloriously liberated.

They danced in front of the fire, first to "Lido" and then to Derek and the Dominos, the original version of "Layla." They danced in wonderful abandonment to four more songs until—laughing—they both collapsed near the fireplace in breathless exhaustion.

Melissa's breath caught at the sudden flare of hunger in Nick's green eyes. Her exhaustion was replaced with a rush of exhilaration. The radio was playing "Cherish" by the Association, and that's what Nick was doing, cherishing her with his look. And then with his lips, as they lowered to hers—asking not demanding, promising not plundering.

But restraint was quickly abandoned as she responded with shy eagerness. Sinking onto the pillows strewn across the floor, Melissa closed her eyes and felt herself sinking into a welcoming haze of emotion. The drumbeat of passion was pounding through her veins, clouding her thoughts and directing her actions.

That first kiss blended into a second, which was twice as hungry, twice as fiery. She slid her fingers over the angular planes of his cheeks and jaw as if wanting to memorize every inch of his face. Her mouth throbbed from his delicious assault as his lips returned again and again to nibble and seduce.

She could feel the banked tension in him as he pressed her even farther into the welcoming softness of the pillows.

Nick's body, blanketing hers, emanated more heat than the fireplace. His hands, stealing beneath her camisole, branded her with their tenderness and seduced her with their creativity.

The first touch of his caressing fingertips on her bare breast made her gasp with startled appreciation. He wielded magic with those long fingertips of his, skimming the smooth surface of her skin before cupping her with a lover's hand. He brushed his thumb over the taut tip until she was completely awash with pleasure.

While he stole her breath with one hand, Nick used the other to undo the buttons of the shirt he'd loaned her, opening it with bold impatience. Freeing her arms, he slowed his movements to a crawl as he gently lifted her satin camisole. The friction of the satiny material dragging over her sensitized skin was magnified by the naked hunger of his appraisal. His eyes remained on hers as he lifted the top millimeter by millimeter. She watched the firelight playing over the planes of his face, mirroring the fire of passion in his eyes as he finally slid his gaze down her body.

She could hardly breathe for the excitement, the anticipation. His visual seduction was heady and filled with promise. Once her breasts were finally bared, he lowered his head and took her into his mouth, his lips closing around the rosy peak, his tongue feathering her nipple.

Ecstasy shot through her, consuming the remnants of her control and instigating a fire storm of wanton gratification. She shifted her legs at the pulses of bliss throbbing between them. Nick shifted with her, arching his back and rubbing the placket of his jeans against her. The ensuing friction was enough to make her moan at the building tension.

Sliding her fingers through his hair, she held him to her as he continued his wicked ways. The passage of his hands and mouth over her body was accomplished with tender skill and naughty imagination.

She wanted . . . no, she needed more. She shifted her fingers from the distraction of his hair to the hem of his T-shirt, tugging it over his head. He did the same with her camisole top, tossing it over his shoulder as she lay on the opened shirt.

Now his bare skin brushed hers without any interference. He settled over her, fitting to her curves as if made for that purpose. She could feel the pounding of his heart against her breast as he kissed her deeply, the thrust of his tongue engaging hers in a reckless tussle that ended with both of them surrendering in delight.

His kisses spilled onto her face, chasing over her eyes, teasing her ears, sliding down her neck to dip in the hollow of her collarbone only to return to her mouth and start all over again. This time when he reached her ears, he paused to dally, nibbling on her earlobe and whispering dark promises of delight. His moist breath ricocheted off her skin and sent shivers of joy down her spine. Her bare feet curled in delight at his lusty teasing.

When his hand shifted to her leg, beneath her skirt, Melissa could only think how right it felt. And how he was able to create magic with his touch, leaving a trail of meteoric persuasion behind. She was lost in the moment as his fingers moved past her knee to the softness of her thigh, ever closer to the source of her feminine heat.

Only then did Nick realize she wasn't wearing any underwear. He wasn't able to resist brushing the crispness of her hair with his thumb, cupping his hand against her mound.

Gasping, she jackknifed into a sitting position, coming to her senses with the speed of someone who'd just been doused with cold water. For one split second his hand was trapped in the inner folds of her dewy warmth before she skittered away from him like a nervous rabbit.

Shaking her head, she tried to speak, but no words would come out. Instead she grabbed the white shirt, stuffing her arms into it and wrapping it around her as she lurched to her feet. A second later she'd bolted.

Swearing under his breath, Nick followed her outside, but she'd already taken off down his drive, and somehow he knew she wouldn't appreciate him coming after her. The rain had stopped, and she'd managed to slip into her sandals before taking off. She had her tote bag slung over her arm, too.

Returning to his living room, he caught sight of something she'd left behind. And he knew what he had to do. Because he also knew Lissa—knew she'd try to deny what happened between them. But he wasn't about to let her.

Because he'd never shared with a woman what he'd just shared with her. She'd gotten to him. He'd never felt this way about anyone before, and he wasn't about to let her get away now.

So it was that Nick sauntered into the library shortly before closing time on Tuesday, holding Melissa's purple camisole in his hand—like a knight wearing his lady's colors—while boldly proclaiming, "Lissa, you left this behind the other night...."

Six

Melissa froze. This couldn't be happening. She must be having a dream. A very bad dream. A nightmare.

She closed her eyes, willing herself to wake up. Her eyes shot open at the sound of Mrs. Cantrell's nervous, tittering laughter. This was *no* dream! Nick still stood there, with her purple camisole dangling suggestively from his index finger.

Melissa snatched it from him before realizing she should have denied any knowledge of the incriminating piece of evidence. "It was raining," she heard herself babbling. "I got wet. That storm yesterday... You remember it, Mrs. Cantrell, right?"

Mrs. Cantrell was too stunned to do more than nod.

Melissa nervously rushed on. "I had to change into dry clothes at Nick's cabin and I just left this behind."

"In front of the fireplace," Nick supplied.

Melissa stared daggers at him before turning her gaze to Mrs. Cantrell. "I got cold. You remember how the temperature dropped after the storm, right?"

"I found it hanging from the edge of the lampshade on the horseshoe floor lamp," Nick confided to Mrs. Cantrell. "And as I recall, the temperature actually was *raised* by a few hundred degrees after that momentous storm." His smile was a study of male complacency and said things that made Melissa blush beet red.

"The library is closing in two minutes," Melissa stated between clenched teeth.

"What's going on in here?" Wayne demanded as he entered the library.

It was all Melissa could do not to sink behind the circulation counter in dismay. "Nothing. The library is closing now."

"I just came to return something of Melissa's," Nick said expansively.

"A piece of lovely purple lingerie," Mrs. Cantrell piped up.

"What the hell were you doing with Melissa's lingerie?" Wayne demanded, his face turning a purple only a few shades lighter than said piece of lingerie.

"You figure it out," Nick laconically replied. "I'll see you later, Lissa," he said with a slow and intimate smile. Seconds later he was gone, leaving Melissa to deal with Mrs. Cantrell and Wayne.

"The library is closed," she briskly informed them both.

"Of course," Mrs. Cantrell said, rushing out of the building. Melissa hadn't seen the older woman move that fast in years.

"Are you going to tell me what's going on here?" Wayne demanded.

Looking down at her clenched hand, Melissa realized she was still holding the incriminating camisole.

"The library is closed!" Melissa cried out to the newcomer who'd just opened the door.

"I don't care if it is," Alberta Beasley declared. "I just passed Mrs. Cantrell outside and she was going on about Melissa's purple lingerie hanging from Nick Grant's horseshoe lampshade. The woman has clearly gone off her rocker! I never heard such a ridiculous story, and I told her so. As if poor Melissa would wear purple lingerie! She's much too...sensible. Why, the poor girl has enough to contend with without this kind of story going around."

"I agree. That's why I'm trying to find out what's going on," Wayne said.

Melissa didn't say a word. She knew if she opened her mouth, she'd get into trouble. She was already furious with Nick, and now Alberta was adding fuel to the fire with her obvious belief that Melissa was incapable of wearing sexy lingerie. Sensible, was she?

"The library is closed," Melissa repeated, grabbing the key to lock up and corralling Alberta and Wayne so that they had to step toward the door or get mowed down.

"I'm not going anywhere until I find out what happened," Alberta stubbornly maintained.

"What happened? I'll tell you what happened. I put my trousseau to good use," Melissa angrily shot back.

"Oh, my stars!" Alberta exclaimed. "With Nick Grant? Melissa, how could you? We're all going to end up on *America's Most Wanted.*"

"For leaving my camisole at Nick's cabin?" Melissa countered. "I don't think so."

"The man isn't who he claims he is," Alberta angrily maintained.

"What's she talking about?" Wayne demanded.

"Nothing," Melissa said as Alberta stalked off in a huff. "She just has an active imagination."

"What about Grant?" Wayne retorted. "Does he have an active imagination, too? Was he lying about what happened at that cabin?"

"I can't talk about this right now, Wayne," she said, putting her hand on his barrel chest and practically pushing him out the door. "The library is closed!"

"I'm not done talking to you," Wayne angrily shouted through the closed and locked door.

"Later, Wayne," she shouted back, heaving a sigh of relief as she heard him walking away.

Melissa couldn't deal with Wayne because she had to deal with Nick first. Nick lingerie-dangling-from-his-fingertips Grant, the man who claimed he was on her side, the man she wanted to throttle.

"I'm going to kill him," Melissa muttered as she turned out the lights, grabbed her purse and headed for the back door—purple camisole still clenched in her left hand.

She drove to Nick's cabin in record time. He was sitting on one of the director's chairs on the front porch, bare feet propped on the railing, waiting for her with a can of beer in his hand.

She stormed right up to him and knocked his feet off the railing. "How could you do that? I've never been so humiliated in my entire life! I thought you were supposed to be helping me! Instead, you've ruined everything!"

"Come now, Lissa. You're exaggerating," Nick calmly replied. Instead of being angry or upset at her ranting and raving, he smiled at her approvingly.

"I am *not* exaggerating," she shot back. "What possessed you to say what you did in front of Wayne?"

"I was trying to make him jealous. It worked, too. Did you see the expression on his face?"

"I most certainly did. He's furious with me. Wayne and I will never reconcile at this rate! We had a fight over it. I had to lock him out of the library."

"Did he try to hurt you?" Nick demanded, leaping to his feet, his lackadaisical air instantly replaced with a protective anger on her behalf.

"No, of course he didn't try to hurt me. He was just trying to find out what was going on."

Nick relaxed his stance. "So what did you tell him?"

"I couldn't tell him anything. I was too upset to talk to him."

"What's the matter, Lissa?" he challenged her. "Afraid he might see the *real* you?"

"What are you talking about?"

"I'm talking about the fact that you shouldn't have to put on this show of being calm and quiet, of being a good girl when really you're hell on wheels and should be damn proud of it."

"The same way my mother was hell on wheels?"

"Of course not. You're *not* your mother. You're *you!* And you should be able to be yourself, especially around people you claim you love. Listen, Emerson said it best. 'It's easy to live for others...I call on you to live for yourself.' That's what I'm doing, Lissa. Calling on you to live for yourself."

"I *am* living for myself. Who else would I be living for?"

"For Wayne."

"If that's the case, then I would have stayed and talked to him instead of coming out here and yelling at you!" she angrily replied.

"You didn't stay because you didn't want him to see the real you."

"I told you already, I left because I was too upset to talk to him."

"Even if he wanted to talk you into coming back to him?" Nick pressed. "That's probably what he wanted to talk to you about, you know."

"I doubt that."

"I don't. What would you say if he does want you back? Would you actually take the jerk back?" Nick frowned at her in disbelief.

His attitude stung. "I love Wayne. Of course I want him back," Melissa stubbornly maintained.

"Be careful what you wish for," Nick told her angrily, his voice a low growl. "You might get it."

"That was the entire purpose of our plan, remember?" she challenged him. "For me to get Wayne back."

"That was before we practically made love last night. Or have you forgotten what it was like? I can tell you that I haven't. I remember every second. Every touch. Every kiss. Maybe I should remind you." Without further ado, he hauled her into his arms.

There were no gentle preliminaries leading up to his kiss. There was no softness to dilute his anger. But there was hunger and there was honesty, as his mouth devoured hers with unmitigated passion. It was a kiss in its most intensely concentrated form—impassioned, direct, compelling, irresistible.

He took a shortcut directly to her heart, bypassing the logic of her mind and appealing to the uncontrollable elements of her darkest needs and desires, of her secret hopes and dreams. He spoke to her with the silky thrusts of his tongue, and she was on the verge of responding, melting in his arms even as he angrily pushed her away.

Nick's green eyes glittered with emotion. "You want that stupid jerk Wayne, then fine! I'll make damn sure you get him."

Her eyes narrowed in a look that was pure Lissa. Without saying a word, she stormed off, her car spitting gravel as she gunned it out of his driveway.

Shoving his shaking hand through his long hair, Nick dropped into the director's chair. He'd wanted Lissa to show her true self, to express her emotions instead of suppressing them—and in doing so he'd opened a Pandora's box of trouble. Because Nick wanted her for himself. He didn't want to just be her buddy or her pal. He wanted to be her lover. So much that it hurt.

Yet she'd made it clear she still loved Wayne. Her claim had been hard for him to acknowledge. It ripped into his soul, reminding him why he'd kept his emotional distance from people over the years. Because when he did feel, it was too damn painful. And it did no good. It didn't change facts.

Besides, Nick reminded himself, he was certainly no prize for her—a man with some money in the bank but no love in his life. A man who didn't know if he was even capable of loving anyone, a man who'd given up trying to unravel his tangled emotions.

Okay, so the more he was with her, the more he knew he didn't want to go back to the city. He wanted to stay with her. Yet, practically speaking, there weren't enough opportunities in a small rural town like Greely for him to make a living as an architect. The bottom line was that he was about to start his professional life all over again and there wasn't a lot of security involved in that kind of move.

While Lissa deserved better than Wayne, Nick felt she also deserved better than *him*. He'd rather cut off his right arm than hurt her.

So it came down to this, Nick noted with brooding deliberation. He was torn between wanting her for himself and wanting to make her happy—even if it took Wayne to do

that. The idea made him sick, but he didn't see that he had
much choice. Lissa deserved to be happy.

Melissa was curled up on her couch, in her favorite
thinking pose, the window air conditioner blowing right in
her face—and still she couldn't get cool. Her face burned at
the memory of Nick's kiss. He was right. Her reaction to his
kiss today and to their embrace last night wasn't that of a
woman in love with another man. She'd responded to him.
Heck, she'd practically melted all over him.

What was happening to her? What was wrong with her?
She was so confused. She couldn't even chalk her reaction
to Nick up to hormonal overdrive. There was more to it than
that. Which scared her even more. This wasn't just a physical attraction. This was *real* trouble.

Magic jumped onto the arm of the couch, stumbling onto
Melissa's lap. Melissa could empathize with her cat's unsteadiness. She hadn't felt like she was on solid ground for
weeks. Yet there had been moments of pure contentment
with Nick, moments of comfort, of barefoot freedom. And
moments of pleasure so intense it made her heart stop just
thinking about it.

Picking up a magazine, she waved it at her flushed face
while Magic settled down on her lap. Melissa was so distracted by her thoughts of Nick that she entirely forgot
about Patty coming over for a night of video-watching and
pizza-eating until her friend showed up at her front door.

"You look surprised to see me," Patty noted. "Something wrong?"

"No. Yes. Come on in."

"I brought two videos. *Last of the Mohicans* and *The
Firm*. That sound okay?"

"Fine," Melissa said absently.

"And I've got Tom Cruise stopping by later," Patty added.

"That's nice."

Patty sighed. "Okay, what's wrong? Is it Wayne again?"

Melissa shook her head. "It's complicated."

"Your life always is," Patty said with the candor of a longtime friend.

"Yeah, it seems that way, doesn't it," Melissa ruefully admitted. "And I don't want complicated, you know? I want simple."

"You're not simple. *You're* complicated. I think you'd get bored with simple."

"It sounds pretty good about now. I think being jilted has affected my brain cells."

"You know, I read an article in a magazine that said you shouldn't call it being jilted. You should say you're going through a *relationship adjustment,*" Patty told her.

"I'm going through *lots* of relationship adjustments," Melissa muttered.

"Lots? What is it specifically that we're talking about here?"

"Nick."

"Ah."

"What's that mean?"

"Nothing. Just that I've seen him at the drugstore a few times. We don't get many men like that here in Greely."

"Men like what?"

"Complicated," Patty said with a grin. "So come on, tell me about you and Nick."

"You already know that we were buddies when we were kids."

Patty nodded. "I also know that he returned your purple camisole to you at the library. Mrs. Cantrell stopped by the drugstore this afternoon, and she claims it was hanging from his lampshade."

"I still can't believe he had the nerve to actually do that. I could have killed him! I'm still furious with him."

"So how did your camisole end up in Nick's possession?"

"You remember that thunderstorm on Sunday? Well, we were out on the lake and got caught in the rain. We both got soaked. I changed into dry clothes at his house."

"Sounds innocent enough."

Melissa guiltily looked away.

"There's more, isn't there?" Patty noted astutely. "Okay, come on. Spill the beans."

"He kissed me. In front of the fireplace."

"And?"

"And one thing led to another . . . and it was incredible."

"You mean you two . . ."

"No, we didn't make love, but it came darn close. Too darn close. Patty, I was supposed to be marrying Wayne, and instead I was making out with Nick!"

"You could do worse," Patty replied with a grin.

"I'm serious."

"So am I. Okay, so you're starting to have feelings for Nick. Are you sure you're not just on the rebound from Wayne?"

"I'm not sure of anything right now," Melissa muttered, shoving her bangs out of her eyes.

"How about Nick? How does he feel about you?"

"I don't know. He's trying to help me out of a rough situation. We devised this plan as a way of getting people to stop feeling sorry for me. As a way of distracting all the gossip from my being 'poor Melissa.'"

"Well, you've certainly done that. Now you're that wild woman Melissa."

"I don't need any more scandal attached to my name, thank you very much!"

"I was only kidding. You know you're well respected in this town. Why do you think everyone was so shocked that Wayne did what he did?"

"Because he's a popular person here in town."

"So are you."

"I don't know about that."

"I do. So what are you saying, that Nick was just being helpful, just lending his support to a friend in need? Doesn't sound like his feelings are strictly Platonic to me, Melissa."

"What should I do?"

"How should I know?"

"What would you do if you were me?"

Patty shifted uncomfortably. "I'm not you."

"What would you do if you were in my position?"

"I don't know. I don't know if I could ever trust Wayne again after doing what he did."

Melissa realized that Patty was voicing an inner fear of her own, one she'd tried to keep down. "Nick thinks I'm an idiot for even considering taking Wayne back," she admitted.

"Love makes people idiots."

"Yes, but I'm not sure I love Wayne the way I did," Melissa wailed. "Otherwise, why would I be having these feelings for Nick?"

"Because he's good-looking?"

"It's so much more than that. When I'm with him, I feel . . ." Melissa shook her head, unable to express it in words. "There are so many things. I can be myself with him, you know? I can yell at him, I can laugh with him, I can be quiet with him."

"I'm sure you were very quiet in front of that fireplace," Patty teased her.

Melissa good-naturedly socked Patty's arm. "That's not what I meant."

"I know. But I don't think we're going to solve this problem in one night, and I'm starving. When's the pizza going to get here?"

Melissa put her hand to her mouth. "Uh-oh. I forgot to order it."

"Great. Some hostess you are."

"I'll make it up to you."

"How?"

"We'll start out with an appetizer of chocolate-chocolate-chip ice cream while we wait for the pizza to get here."

"Sounds like a plan to me!"

After consuming the ice cream and the pizza and viewing *Last of the Mohicans,* Patty wiped away the tears as Melissa rewound the video. "What a kiss." She sighed. "And that waterfall scene...talk about romantic. 'I *will* find you,'" she quoted from the film, sighing again. "Where are the men like that?"

"In the movies," Melissa dryly noted.

Patty remained undaunted. "Did you notice that Nick kind of looks like Daniel Day-Lewis did in that movie? Nick's hair isn't as long, but they both have a similar build. Same kind of angular face. And he certainly has that air of self-containment. The kind of man who's not a follower. The kind of man to forge his own paths. You know Nick better than I do. Is that an accurate description?"

"Very accurate," Melissa softly acknowledged.

"Oh, Melissa." Patty shook her head at her friend's dreamy expression. "What are you going to do?"

It was Melissa's turn to sigh. "I don't have a clue."

* * *

Wayne was waiting for her when she arrived at the library the next morning. His expression wasn't a welcoming one.

"Wayne, I don't want to jeopardize my job by taking care of private affairs during business hours," she told him.

"*Affairs* being the key word here," Wayne retorted. "I tried to see you last night, but Patty stayed at your house until late. Besides, I thought there would be less talk if I saw you in a public place. I figure there's enough talk about you already."

His condemning, judgmental tone of voice set her teeth on edge. "Listen, you were the one who walked out on our engagement," she angrily reminded him as she flicked on the library's lights. "You chose Rosie. What I do is no longer any concern of yours."

"Of course it's my concern," Wayne insisted, following in her footsteps. "You were my fiancée. What you do reflects on me."

She angrily rounded on him. "Oh, that's just great! And what you do reflects on me, Wayne. Running away with Rosie ten days before you were supposed to marry me sure as hell didn't make a good impression!"

"It's not like you to swear, Mel," he said in a disapproving voice.

"How would you know?"

"What kind of thing is that to say?" he countered, looking wounded at her question. "Of course I know. I've known you for three years. I think I know you pretty well."

"I thought I knew you pretty well, too, Wayne," she said quietly. "And the man I knew would never have done what you did."

He shifted uncomfortably. "I told you I was sorry things worked out the way they did."

"Sorry doesn't cut it, Wayne."

"What do you want from me?"

For things to be the way they were before, she thought. Uncomplicated. Safe. Simple. Dependable.

But how dependable could things have been if he left her almost at the altar? It only went to show that things you thought were reliable weren't. She would have thought that Nick was reliable, that he'd never have sabotaged her the way he had.

"Look, Mel, I'm all mixed up right now," Wayne confessed in a low voice. "So much has been happening, you know?"

Sighing, she nodded. "I know."

"I'm sorry I jumped down your throat the way I did. About Grant, I mean. It's just that the thought of you being with him...it's hard for me to swallow, Mel. I won't lie about that. I've still got feelings for you."

"You do?"

"Of course I do. I'm not an inhuman jerk, despite what folks might think. They're all on your side in this thing, you know. They think I'm the bad guy in this scenario, and they're probably right. But I didn't think it would be right to marry you when I had feelings for Rosie."

She noticed his use of the past tense.

"I just want you to be happy, Mel," he said, touching his finger to her cheek. A moment later he was gone.

Melissa felt tears coming to her eyes and quickly blinked them away. First Nick wanted her to be happy and now Wayne wanted her to be happy, too. Which was all very well and good, if she could only decide what it was that *would* make her happy.

She hated these doubts eating away at her. She felt consumed by them. Just when it looked as if she was making progress with Wayne, she began wondering if she really wanted him back after all. How shallow could she get?

This wasn't like her. She wasn't a shallow person. How could it be that three weeks ago she'd been blindly in love with Wayne? And yet now she was starting to have feelings for Nick, feelings that went way above and beyond those of friendship. How could she trust her judgment in these circumstances?

"What a mess," she muttered.

"I agree," Alberta briskly said from the other side of the circulation desk. "I can't believe how people can leave their books laying all over the place this way. Did you get that criminology book in yet?"

"I haven't had time to check the interlibrary loan delivery the driver left last night. Hold on a minute, I'll look." Melissa opened the book-return slot and removed the package from the library system. "Yes, here it is."

"Wonderful!" Alberta pounced on the book the second Melissa finished processing the paperwork and handed it over. Skimming though the table of contents, Alberta jabbed her finger at the chapter entitled Fingerprinting. "Perfect!" Alberta slammed the volume closed and clutched it to her bosom. "Thank you for getting this for me, my dear," she said, turning to leave. "I'll see you tomorrow."

"Aren't you forgetting something?" Melissa reminded her. Seeing the other woman's confused expression, Melissa added, "You need to check the book out."

"Oh, right. Of course. I don't know where my mind was." Alberta returned to the desk and reluctantly handed the book back before digging in her pocketbook for her library card. "Have you seen Nick today?"

"No."

"You be careful with him, Melissa. He's not like the boys around here. He's got strange ideas and notions."

And he kisses like the devil. The provocative thought shot through Melissa's head like lightning across a summer sky.

"Mark my words, no good will come of him being here," Alberta proclaimed before taking her book and Melissa's peace of mind along with it.

Melissa welcomed the scheduled story hour she had planned for that afternoon, because it was impossible for her to brood about her own situation when she had to amuse and amaze fifteen two- to five-year-olds. Reading aloud to them required her full attention.

This was one of her favorite parts of her job—watching the children as they learned about the magic of books and the stories they contained. The group of children sat around her on the sturdy indoor-outdoor carpeting she'd sweet-talked an area merchant into donating. Today she was reading *Where the Wild Things Are,* and the kids stared at her wide-eyed as she dramatically read all the roles, changing her voice with each one.

By the time Melissa closed up at the end of the day, she felt like she'd gotten a lot of work accomplished. Aside from the successful story hour, she'd compiled last week's circulation records, processed a new stack of interlibrary loan requests and drawn up the flier for the library's annual book drive next month.

The truth was that her job had been a lifeline for her during this traumatic time, giving her a sense of structure in a life suddenly gone awry. Now more than ever, she needed that structure—because her world had been turned upside down and her love for Wayne put in question by her growing feelings for Nick.

* * *

"How kind of you to accept our invitation to tea," Beatrice told Nick with a fluttery wave of her handkerchief. She was wearing gloves, the dainty white kind that Victorian ladies had worn.

"You said there was something you needed to tell me about Melissa," Nick reminded her, recalling that the invitation had actually been more like a royal command.

"That's right. Do come in. Sit down."

Nick gingerly sat on a dainty love seat that reminded him of the driver's seat in a subcompact he'd rented once. Then, as now, his knees ended up practically under his chin.

"You and Alberta can have a little chat while I get the tray for our tea," Beatrice declared.

When Alberta fixed him with her eagle eye, Nick made no move to look away. The old bird was definitely up to something. "So what was it you wanted to tell me about Melissa?" he inquired.

"In time, my good fellow," she said with a regal wave of her white-gloved hand, reminding Nick of Queen Elizabeth. "You young people are in such a rush these days. Comes from living in the city, I suppose. Which city did you say you live in?"

"I didn't say."

"Why not? Are you trying to hide something?"

Nick shifted on the couch, searching for a more comfortable position. Clearly this was going to be a long visit. "I live in Chicago."

"How nice for you. And what is it you do there?"

"I'm an architect."

"An architect. How exciting. So you know all about the work of Mies Van der Rohe, then? And Frank Lloyd Wright? I visited Chicago once and saw their work. Mies Van der Rohe designed the Sears Tower in Chicago, right?"

"Wrong." Nick held back a smile at this blatant attempt to trip him up. "The Sears Tower was designed by the architectural firm of Skidmore, Owings and Merrill."

"Oh. But of course, being from Chicago yourself, you'd know that. What do your parents do?"

"Not much," Nick laconically replied. "They're retired."

"And before they retired?" Alberta pressed.

Nick was prevented from answering by the arrival of Beatrice. He gallantly got up and carried the heavy tray for her.

"Thank you," Beatrice murmured gratefully, before sinking into a doily-covered armchair. "Just set it here on the coffee table. Now how would you like your tea, Nick? With milk or with lemon?"

"Milk."

After handing him his tea, she asked, "Sugar?" She held out the ornate silver-plated sugar bowl.

He took two spoonfuls. The dainty-looking teacup and saucer looked lost in his big hands. He felt all thumbs as he sipped the tea, scalding his mouth in the process.

"Oh, it's too hot, I should have told you," Beatrice said in apology.

"Here." Alberta removed the teacup and saucer and thrust a glass of cold water into his hand. "Drink this."

He gulped half the glass down.

"There now. I'll just take that out of your way." Alberta took the glass, handling it as if it were a priceless heirloom. In fact, she took it clear into the kitchen.

"I'm sorry about this," Beatrice apologized again, looking truly remorseful.

Nick was sorry, too. His tongue was numb. He wasn't sure he'd be able to taste anything for a week. All this to get some information about Melissa, information that the Beasley sisters were in no hurry to impart.

To his surprise there were no questions about the incident in the library the other day, when he'd returned Melissa's purple lingerie. In fact, Alberta stayed away from the subject of his relationship with Melissa. Instead she seemed much more interested in his past.

As the inquisition continued for another hour, Nick couldn't resist asking a question of his own. "Are any of your relatives from Spain, by any chance?" he inquired dryly.

"Of course not," Alberta replied with a disapproving sniff. "Our ancestors came to Illinois with Morris Berkbeck from England in the early 1800s. They were among the first to settle in this area. In fact, this town would have been called Beasley instead of Greely were it not for the fact that Goose Greely put his name on the incorporation papers first."

"His real name was Vermillion Greely," Beatrice inserted. "His nickname was Goose."

"Because he didn't have the sense God gave a goose," Alberta maintained.

"He was smart enough to get the town named after him," Beatrice pointed out.

"Only because he cheated," Alberta stated.

"But we're straying from the point," Beatrice said. "Whatever made you ask if we were from Spain, Nick?"

"Your interrogation routine," Nick reluctantly confessed.

"I just read a book about the Spanish Inquisition," Beatrice noted. "The hero saved the heroine at the last moment—"

"Oh, do stop blathering, sister," Alberta snapped. To Nick, she stiffly said, "I'm sorry if our questions have offended you, Mr. Grant. In that case, we won't keep you any longer."

Nick found himself getting the bum's rush as he was shown the door in record time. As the door closed firmly in his face, Nick realized he still didn't know any more about Melissa than he had when he'd arrived. Which made him wonder if he'd just been conned by a pair of pros.

To Melissa's relief, the past two days had been relatively quiet, allowing her to concentrate on work. Neither Nick nor Wayne nor the Beasley sisters had showed up at the library during that time. Their absence had provided her with some badly needed breathing space.

Not that she was any closer to knowing what to do about things, because she wasn't. But at least she'd been able to think about something else for a change—including the fact that the annuals she'd planted in front of her house were sadly drooping from lack of water.

It was early evening, and she was outside watering the pink and white geraniums planted beneath the living room's protruding bay window, while her cat avidly watched her every move from said window, when Melissa saw Beatrice walking down the sidewalk. Not wanting to be rude, Melissa waved. After all, it wasn't Beatrice's fault that her older sister tended to be somewhat overbearing. Beatrice waved back, using the lacy handkerchief she always kept with her.

"My, those poor geraniums of yours look a bit wilted," Beatrice noted as she stopped to join Melissa. "And you certainly have your fair share of dandelions this year, don't you?" she added, waving her handkerchief toward the front lawn, which was generously speckled with the yellow flowers. "Legend has it that they're useful for the flow of sperm, you know."

Stunned, Melissa almost dropped the garden hose she was holding. As it was, she let it jerk in her hand, splattering the living room window with water and spooking her cat in the process.

"I do know about the birds and the bees, my dear," Beatrice noted with a grin. "I almost married once, in my youth." Her smile faded. "He was killed in the Second World War. The last day of the war. There was never anyone else for me."

"I'm sorry," Melissa murmured.

Beatrice patted her hand, the one *not* holding the garden hose. "I just wanted you to know that I do know what it's like to lose the man you love. Unless Wayne wasn't *really* the man meant for you. Then that would be an entirely different kettle of fish, indeed. But back to your poor geraniums," Beatrice happily chatted on. "Did you know that pink geraniums are used in love spells while the white ones are said to increase fertility? I picked that up from the romance novel I'm reading—the one that looks as if Nick Grant had posed for the cover. It's a Regency, and he has that air about him, you know. He has the long legs and the lean face. He looked right at home sipping tea when we had him over this afternoon. He stayed for two hours, until Alberta chased him off with her questions."

"You had Nick come to tea? What for?" Melissa knew she sounded abrupt, but she couldn't help herself. The vision of the Beasley sisters grilling poor Nick for two hours was impossible to dismiss.

"What for?" Beatrice's handkerchief fluttered in agitation. "Well, um, I suppose... Why, to be neighborly, of course."

"Beatrice, tell me the truth. Your sister doesn't still believe that Nick is an impostor, does she?"

"I'm not at liberty to say," Beatrice replied. "But I don't think that Nick killed anyone. Oh, dear!" She held her handkerchief to her mouth in dismay. "I shouldn't have said that. Don't tell Alberta I did, or she'll have a hissy fit, to be sure. She's convinced that Nick must have killed off the real Nick and taken his place. After all, Mrs. Abinworth's nephew was such a scrawny little thing. And there's nothing scrawny about Nick Grant now."

"Trust me, Beatrice. He's the same Nick, just with a different appearance."

"You know how Alberta is. She loves a good mystery."

"And if there isn't a good mystery, she'll invent one," Melissa muttered.

"Well, that, too," Beatrice had to agree.

"Is that why she wanted that book on criminology I got for her?" Melissa demanded. "Because she wanted to experiment on Nick?" A flash of Alberta's finger jabbing at the table of contents came back to her. "Fingerprinting!"

Beatrice jumped guiltily.

"Oh, Beatrice, you and Alberta didn't try fingerprinting Nick, did you?"

"It wasn't my idea," Beatrice maintained, dabbing her handkerchief at the beads of sweat dotted along her upper lip.

"What did you two do? Try to stick his finger in an ink pad? Take a mug shot?"

"Of course not. Our manners aren't as bad as all that," Beatrice protested in a huff. "We got his fingerprints on a glass. In fact, Alberta is on her way to the sheriff's office with it right now!"

Seven

"The sheriff's office!" Melissa exclaimed. "Why did she do that?"

"Because the sheriff is the only one who can investigate those fingerprints."

"And what is Alberta's excuse for needing this information? Surely she doesn't think she can just waltz into the sheriff's office and demand that he trace Nick's fingerprints?"

"You're forgetting, my dear, that Sheriff Edelman was in Alberta's kindergarten class. I think he's always been a little afraid of her. With good reason," Beatrice added. "You know how she can get."

Melissa groaned. "I can't believe you did this to Nick."

"Well, if he hasn't done anything, then there's no harm done," Beatrice pointed out.

"You can't go inviting someone to your home just so you can fingerprint him!"

"That wasn't the *only* reason. We wanted to ask him some questions, too."

"Oh, Beatrice." Melissa shook her head.

The older woman hung her head in discomfort as she confessed, "I felt so badly when he burned his tongue on that hot tea. But it was the only way to be sure and get him to drink from the glass of cold water. I drew the line at taking blood, though."

"You tell your sister to keep her hands off Nick," Melissa declared vehemently. "Or she'll answer to me!"

"I don't think that's going to scare her, Melissa," Beatrice timidly replied.

"That's only because she hasn't seen me angry before," Melissa muttered darkly. "But that could change if she pulls another stunt like this. Tell her that, Beatrice."

"I will, dear."

"And I want you to promise to come tell me if your sister gets any more bright ideas."

"Bright ideas? Well, she did try to get that high-powered telescope she's been wanting for years, but it's still on back order from the catalog company. They said they wouldn't get it in until September."

"Thank heavens for that. Remember, Beatrice. You keep me posted if Alberta tries any more spying activities, and I'll make sure you have all the wonderful romances you can imagine to read for the next year!"

Beatrice beamed. "Why, thank you, dear. I'll do my best." After the older woman left, Melissa stored the garden hose in the garage and decided to pay Nick a visit. She needed to warn him about the Beasley sisters, and Alberta in particular.

She grimaced at the thought of Nick being grilled for two hours by a relentless Alberta. And all because of her. He didn't deserve this. He certainly didn't deserve to be investigated by the sheriff, for heaven's sake. She had to warn him.

Melissa found Nick down by the lake, skipping stones across the smooth surface of the water. She'd taught him how to do that when they'd been kids. They'd even gone on to have contests, with Melissa winning most of them until the end of his stay, when his throwing skills had vastly improved.

"You're holding the stone too tightly," she told him. "You need to relax more when you throw."

"Sounds like old times," Nick murmured mockingly, rolling a new stone between his long fingers as he silently acknowledged that what he felt for Melissa was more than the fondness of an old friend. These were new times, and his feelings for her were equally new. As for relaxing, he hadn't been able to do that since she'd stormed off a few days ago.

He'd decided to give her some time on her own. For the one who was supposed to be seeing clearly in this twosome, he certainly wasn't behaving like it. She said she loved Wayne. Why was that so hard for him to accept, let alone to believe? Because it hurt too damn much.

Picking up a smooth pebble, Melissa joined him. "I'd like to talk to you," she said, throwing the stone over the water, where it skipped three times before sinking.

"Talk away."

"I understand that the Beasley sisters invited you to tea this afternoon."

"That's right."

"Did they give you a hard time?"

"I survived."

"I'm sorry."

"Sorry that I survived?" he inquired dryly.

"No, of course not. I meant I'm sorry that you had to go through that."

He turned to face her. "I didn't *have* to do anything. I chose to go over there."

"I don't think you realized what you were getting into when you accepted their invitation. Did you know they fingerprinted you?"

"That explains the white gloves," he murmured. Seeing her look, he added, "They were both wearing white gloves. I thought it meant the tea was formal. Now I realize what they were up to. But why on earth would they want my fingerprints?"

"To see if you're really Nick Grant. I'm told Alberta is over at the sheriff's office right now."

To Melissa's surprise, Nick cracked up.

"It's not funny," she said.

"It certainly isn't," he noted with a slow smile, his eyes crinkling a little at the corners. "Now everyone will know that I've got two speeding tickets on my record. That's about all she'll find out."

"I can't believe she did this. I'm sorry. You don't need this trouble. You came down here to get some thinking done, and instead you're being fingerprinted by a pair of suspicious neighbors."

"Just out of curiosity, why don't they believe I'm who I say I am?"

"Because you're so different."

Nick nodded, his sharp features taking on a brooding expression. "Amazing how many people judge a book by its cover. Doesn't matter what's inside. It's all image. All perception. And it changes the way people look at you, the way they treat you."

"Not the way *everyone* treats you," she denied.

"You didn't recognize me, either."

"Not at first, no. Twenty years is a long time, Nick. You didn't recognize me, either," she reminded him.

"Not until you shoved that pie in my chest. When I saw that look of murder in your eyes, I knew it was you."

His expression started out as a rueful one, but was soon transformed into one of familiar intent as his direct gaze fastened on hers. She could only partially translate the message she saw written in his eyes. She didn't know the answer to the questions she saw there. She only knew that when he looked at her that way, her heart sang, her toes curled and her mind turned to mush. Shaken, she tore her eyes away.

"So what do we do now?" she asked somewhat breathlessly.

"Continue with the plan," Nick replied. "Does the town still put on a big Fourth of July bash?"

Melissa nodded.

"We should go together."

She should get her head examined. The thought slipped through her mind even as she said, "Okay."

What exactly was she doing here? The plan had seemed simple at first. Nick coming to her rescue, preventing the gossips in town from labeling her "poor Melissa" again. Great. That had worked. Now they'd labeled her as a wild woman fooling around with the town's mystery man.

She'd been avoiding spending much time in town, aside from work, and her nearly empty kitchen cabinets reflected that fact. Now she'd just agreed to attend the town's biggest function with Nick. A move sure to cause more talk.

But her staying home would also cause talk, she firmly reminded herself. And it was time she did what she wanted, instead of what she thought was proper or suitable. Time for her to live for herself.

And so she sat next to Nick as he settled at the end of the dock, dangling his bare feet in the water to cool down in the still mugginess of a summer day. He made no comment as she slipped off her sandals and joined him, although his smile reflected his pleasure at her move.

Time slipped away, and Melissa was left wondering why they couldn't be friends like this all the time, although even now there was an awareness humming through her system. Had she risked ruining her relationship with Nick in her attempts to get Wayne back? Was it worth that risk? At the moment she didn't think so.

But then she was the first to admit that she wasn't thinking clearly—hadn't been for some time now. Why was it so difficult for her to decide what she wanted?

"Penny for your thoughts," Nick offered.

She sighed. "I was just thinking how complicated life gets."

"Maybe this next step in our plan will finally get you what you want," Nick said.

The problem was that Melissa was no longer positive what it was—or more precisely *whom* it was—she truly did want. And that fact scared her almost as much as calling off the wedding had.

Melissa was a nervous wreck two hours before Nick even arrived to pick her up on Independence Day. Her hair refused to behave, and she couldn't decide what to wear. It was going to be another scorcher—temperatures in the low nineties with humidity levels to match. She had her choice of a red tank dress or a Bermuda shorts set in crinkled navy blue cotton.

She'd signed up to man the ticket booth at the fun fair in the park right after the parade, so she'd need something comfortable and washable. She would change for the square dance that evening. She already had tonight's outfit down pat, a red gingham dress with a full skirt that would be perfect for the occasion. Not that she planned on dancing much. But the event was put on by the town fathers, and as the librarian she was expected to show up.

She finally decided to wear the blue shorts set, because it was coolest without showing off too much skin. And the Bermuda shorts had pockets, to hide her hands in should she get nervous—or should she be tempted to throttle anyone, she decided with newfound spunk.

A red cotton scarf wrapped diagonally and tied around her waist served as a belt and added a dash of color. As Melissa leaned toward the mirror to check her eye shadow, Magic batted at the dangling ends of the scarf—almost falling into the sink in the process.

"You *nutzifagen,*" she clucked, steadying the cat, remembering again how Nick's reaction to Magic had been so different from Wayne's. Wayne had always tried to order Magic around, as if she were a dog instead of a cat. He'd tried to control the cat, to no avail.

It made sense that a loner like Nick would appreciate a cat's independence. He was sure enough of himself not to feel threatened when a cat didn't do what he told it to. Now that Melissa thought about it, Nick hadn't tried to tell Magic what to do, he'd simply let her do her thing.

Melissa stared into her cat's eyes as if the feline had just helped her make a major discovery. Indeed, Magic's expression was one of superior indulgence. "Okay, so you like Nick better than Wayne," Melissa acknowledged. "I can't pick the man in my life because my cat likes one better than the other."

Magic haughtily tilted her head, silently demanding, *Why not?*

"It's not logical," Melissa muttered.

Like talking to me is? Melissa could practically see the comment in the feline's expressive eyes.

Nick's arrival interrupted Melissa's conversation with her cat. The denim cutoffs he wore displayed his lean, impossibly long legs. His T-shirt was red. She'd noticed that, contrary to popular fashion, Nick never wore T-shirts that said anything. "I don't need a T-shirt to speak for me," had been his only comment when she'd mentioned it.

He was right. His green eyes spoke more eloquently than any T-shirt could, and their visual message never failed to affect her. They told her the kind of man he was. And they told her that he wanted her. But that wanting was now shadowed with something else. Regret? Her heart caught, as if snagged by a thorn. For once, Nick was the first to look away.

"I'm not quite ready," she murmured as she let him in. "Take a seat, and I'll be done in a minute."

She whirled away in a cloud of honeysuckle cologne. Nick recognized the scent. Honeysuckle grew alongside the cabin, filling his nights with its sweet smell. It was fitting that Melissa wore the same fragrance—one that was haunting in its familiarity.

Melissa had been equally haunting, commandeering his thoughts during his waking hours and his dreams at night. His feelings for her ran deep, even deeper than he'd thought.

A demanding *meow* brought his attention to the cat sitting at his feet. The moment Nick sat on the couch, Melissa's cat jumped onto his lap to perform her ritualistic routine of placing her paws on his shoulder and staring him in the eye. He could have sworn he saw the feline smile before she jumped down and meandered over to a patch of sunlight on the floor.

With a gleam in her eyes, the cat suddenly froze, her black tail swishing restlessly. Instead of pouncing on some toy or imagined plaything, the cat batted at her own moving tail.

As Nick watched in amused disbelief, Magic went on to chase her tail.

Melissa walked in on the middle of Magic's performance. Ruefully shaking her head, she said, "She's four years old, you'd think she'd know that tail belongs to her after all this time."

"There's a Chinese proverb about cats and their tails," Nick murmured. "Something about a kitten chasing its own tail. When the older cat asked why, the kitten replied that it kept its happiness in its tail. Since the kitten wanted to be happy, he chased after it to catch it. The older cat told him that there was no need to chase his tail because his tail was part of him—as was his happiness—and he should carry both proudly rather than chasing after it all the time."

The story hit Melissa, who wondered if *she'd* been chasing after happiness, chasing useless dreams with Wayne rather than enjoying the moments of happiness she had with Nick.

"What are you looking at?" Nick asked, noticing Melissa's gaze fixed on him.

She just smiled and reached out to touch the fading scar near his eye. "It's healing nicely," she noted, letting her fingertips linger to soak up the warmth of his skin.

Their eyes met, and silent questions flew in the energized air between them. Questions neither one had the answers to.

"We'd better go," Nick finally said.

Melissa nodded, reluctantly lowering her hand and smiling at the now familiar humming originating from her fingertips. One thing she was certain of—Nick was lightning to her nervous system...and owner of an ever-growing part of her heart.

Nick kept his hand on her arm as they entered the crowd lining the three-block-long parade route. Greely's business district was barely two blocks long, its 1870s-style store-fronts strung out along Main Street. It was pure Americana, taken straight from a Norman Rockwell illustration or the pages of Sinclair Lewis's classic *Main Street*.

Melissa shot Nick a grin as she led him close to the curb in front of Strohmson's Bakery. "You can't see from back here." She tugged him past the curious stares of Greely's residents, heading for a small opening. "Here. This is perfect." She handed him one of the small American flags that were being passed out. "Look, they're just about to start."

Nick looked, all right, but at her, not at the parade. Greely's Lincoln High School Marching Band could have walked by on their heads for all he noticed. His attention was fixed on Melissa's expressive face.

This was the first time he'd seen her so animated, and only now did he realize how much Wayne's betrayal had hurt her, casting a pall on her zest for life. This was the Lissa he'd dreamed of seeing, the one who laughed and smiled, the one who looked at life with confidence and verve.

She slipped her hand into his as the float carrying Wayne and the winning football team he coached went by. Nick found himself wishing she'd touched him because she'd wanted to, not to teach her ex-fiancé a lesson. But she wasn't looking at Wayne. She was looking at Nick with something new in her eyes. Speculation. "You look like you just swallowed a fish," she teased him.

"I just saw who's on the next float," he said.

"You mean Alberta?" she replied.

Sure enough, Alberta Beasley sat on the Founders' Day float, appropriately ensconced on a throne.

"You don't have to worry about her anymore," Melissa assured him earnestly. "I warned her off."

"That was brave of you," he noted ruefully.

"I told her to keep her hands off you."

"I'm sure relieved to know my virtue is safe from the dastardly Alberta Beasley," he solemnly stated.

Melissa socked his arm. "You know what I mean."

"Yeah, I know what you mean," he said softly, loving this new Melissa. "No one messes with Lissa."

"You got that right," she agreed.

Her grin was a work of art, in his opinion. More beautiful than the lines of a Sullivan building, more inspiring than the airy spires of a Gothic cathedral.

The parade ended with one of the fire trucks from the volunteer fire department, sirens going. Nick's internal sirens were also blaring on full alert. Melissa was an impossible dream.

Like going into business on your own, an inner voice mocked him. He couldn't do both. He didn't have any security to offer her. Besides, she loved Wayne. He'd do well to remember that. Sure he could tempt her, but for how long? He didn't want a quick roll in the hay with her. He wanted to make love to her until the end of the world.

"Parade's over," she told him. "Time to head for the park. I've got to set up the donation box for the library's book drive and then I'm in charge of the ticket booth for the next hour. This year, the library is getting part of the proceeds, money from the Community Chest."

Nick was only human. The mere mention of a chest made him remember the divine softness of hers. His eyes lingered on the open V of her sleeveless navy blouse, where only a demure amount of skin showed. She looked wholesome, an all-American girl ... woman, he quickly revised. There was no mistaking that. Her curves were full, not the immature lines of a girl.

She had her hair done up in some kind of French braid that made him want to undo it and run his fingers through the strands he knew to be incredibly silky and soft. *You've got it bad,* he told himself.

While Melissa did her duty at the ticket booth, Nick wandered around the fairgrounds. "Nicky!" a woman's voice cried out. "Nicky, is that you?" A blowsy blonde rushed up to him.

"I'm sorry, I . . ."

"It's me. Peggy Sue. Peggy Sue Hammond. You remember me, surely."

The woman of his dreams when he'd been eleven and had spied on her bedroom window from his tree fort, hoping to catch a glimpse of her in her black bra. "Hello, Peggy Sue," he replied. "How have you been?"

"Awful, but I don't want to talk about me. I want to talk about you. Look at you." She devoured him with her eyes. "You sure were a late bloomer . . . but, honey, it was worth the wait."

Nick remembered now that subtlety had never been Peggy Sue's strong point.

"Do you know everyone in this little town is talking about you?" Peggy Sue continued. "Of course I make it a practice not to listen to gossip. But I work at the Cut N' Curl on Main Street. Rosie works there, too. So naturally we all knew about the goings-on with her and Wayne. Not that I'm one to throw stones. Lord knows, after two divorces, I'm in no position to pass judgment on others. So what are you doing here in Greely after all this time?"

"Taking some vacation time."

"Honey, no one comes to Greely for a vacation. Most of the folks around here can't wait to shake the mud of this place off their feet."

"Looks like plenty of people have chosen to stay," Nick noted, indicating the large crowd assembled in the park.

"They've come from miles around, and this is the only excitement in their poor lives. We're talking about people who brag about going over to Illiopolis, just so they can say they've been smack dab to the middle of the state. Like it was some big deal or something."

"We're also talking about people who believe in supporting their neighbors in times of trouble, people who look out for each other, who have a strong sense of values and of community," Nick quietly pointed out.

"Why, sure. That's why I've stayed," Peggy Sue claimed, quickly changing her tune. Running her hand up his bare arm, she flirtatiously asked, "Why don't you join me this afternoon and I'll show you how well I could look after you."

"I'm here with Melissa."

Peggy Sue made a moue of dismissal. "She's still head over heels in love with Wayne. She won't notice if you leave."

"Yes, I would," Melissa stated from behind Nick. "Hello, Peggy Sue. Out hunting, are you?"

Peggy Sue stared at Melissa as if she'd grown two horns.

"Nick, I'd like to introduce you to my friend Patty. She's over there waiting for us. Excuse us, Peggy Sue."

"Smooth move," Nick noted with a slow smile.

"The woman is a walking barracuda," Melissa muttered.

"A good-looking barracuda," he noted.

"If you care for the obvious type. Luckily I've got more faith in your good taste than that."

Before Nick could make a comment, Melissa halted in front of Patty. "Nick, I'd like you to meet my best friend, Patty Jensen. Patty, this is Nick Grant."

"You work at the drugstore," Nick noted, offering her his hand.

Patty shyly shook it. "That's right."

Nick would have said more, but he found himself roped in by Mrs. Cantrell, who insisted his presence was needed as an impartial judge for the pie-eating contest.

"That's one of my areas of expertise," Nick said with a meaningful look in Melissa's direction. "Especially blueberry pie."

Left on their own for the moment, Patty and Melissa were able to speak freely. "How are things going?" Patty asked her.

"I could be in serious trouble here," Melissa acknowledged. "I thought I loved Wayne. Now I don't know."

"I read something that might assist you with that," Beatrice inserted with a helpful wave of her handkerchief. "Legend has it . . ."

"Beatrice, I didn't see you standing there," Melissa exclaimed, cutting off the older woman's words. She remembered all too well Beatrice's last legend referring to dandelions!

"There now, dear. No need to blush. This story isn't about sperm."

Patty's jaw dropped open.

"You young people today think you know it all," Beatrice clucked with a shake of her head. "Anyway, in that same herbal book that listed the dandelions, I read something that might help you, Melissa. It said that when a girl is torn between two men, she should take two green leaves from a rosebush—and you've got that nice pink one growing along the fence, although that fence could use painting. But back to the leaves. You take the two rosebush leaves inside and name them, one for Nick, one for Wayne. The leaf that stays green the longest is the one that is truest."

"Beatrice . . ."

"No need to thank me, dear. We romantics have to stick together. Oh, I see dear Mr. Killian over there. I must go have a word with him." Tucking her handkerchief into the belt of her dress, Beatrice moved on.

"What was that all about?" Patty demanded.

"Don't ask."

Since it was Patty's turn to man the ticket booth, Melissa was on her own. Looking around, she tried to see the festivities through Nick's eyes. A variety of activities were scheduled to take place throughout the day—a pie-eating contest, water-balloon fights, a watermelon-eating contest followed shortly by a watermelon-seed-shooting contest, to see who could make the slippery black seeds go the farthest.

At the moment, a heated game of horseshoes was going on over at the horseshoe pit, the metallic clang of a ringer interspersed with the occasional thunk of a horseshoe falling short. The match was a hotly contested one, with a large crowd watching. The older male spectators chewed tobacco while the younger ones chewed wads of gum, enough to make the same bulge in their cheek that their fathers and grandfathers sported.

Denim was the attire of the day. A few of the old-timers wore overalls, while the others wore their Sunday jeans. Melissa smiled as she spotted a T-shirt that said Manure Movers of America. It was worn by Larry Hickman. She'd gone to school with him. In fact, her ties to all of these people went back to her childhood.

They were good people. Decent, hardworking people with caring hearts. When her family had left for California, there had been plenty of volunteers to take care of Melissa. She'd stayed with Patty, whose parents had taken Melissa under their wing, adding her to their brood of five kids as if she were just another one of their own. Until they'd retired to

Florida last winter, they'd continued to have Melissa over for all the holiday events and family gatherings.

And they weren't the only ones. Since her return from college, Melissa never wanted for lack of offers of help—to shovel the snow on her walk, to pitch in when her basement flooded, to bring chicken soup and homemade casseroles when she'd caught the flu.

Greely was home, pure and simple. And it would stay her home, despite what had happened with Wayne. Melissa caught sight of him across the park. He was at the dunking booth, and there was a long line of kids from his high school team trying to dunk him. Despite what she might think of Wayne's loyalty to her, there was no faulting his love for the kids he coached.

But she could sure fault his sense of timing and his cowardly way of skipping town. Knowing exactly what she had to do, Melissa joined the line at the dunking booth. When her turn came up, she saw the startled look in Wayne's eyes a second before she hit the bull's-eye with the ball, knocking Wayne into the tank of water. She grinned in triumph at the strong feeling of satisfaction she felt at having dumped him in the water, as if it was a figurative revenge for his dumping her.

The old Melissa would never have considered dunking him in the first place. She certainly wouldn't have basked in her accomplishment after doing so. No, she'd have felt guilt. But no more.

Turning, she saw that Nick had joined her. For once Nick looked as astonished as Wayne, although Nick's expression quickly turned to one of appreciation.

"Nice throw," he said with a slow smile. A man of few words, that was Nick, Melissa silently noted. But the way he said something often told her as much as the words themselves. His quiet voice was laced with pride and approval as he asked, "What's next on the agenda?"

"Let's eat. Unless being judge of the pie-eating contest turned you off of food? It's not a pretty sight," she noted with a laugh, remembering the contests she'd viewed in the past.

"I'm made of stronger stuff than that," Nick maintained.

They stopped at a yellow-and-white tent covering picnic tables with metal folding chairs. The tent top was held down by ropes, leaving all sides open. The smell of grilling hamburgers and barbecued ribs filled the air. They loaded plates full of food—ribs, bratwurst with sauerkraut, early sweet corn freshly picked.

"Leave enough room for dessert," Melissa said with a grin. "You haven't lived till you've tasted Mrs. Forbes's homemade ice cream."

Nick's reply was forestalled by the sound of Alberta's ringing voice. "There you are. I've been looking all over for you," Alberta stated. "Your secret is out now, Nick Grant. I know you're nothing more than a jailbird!"

Eight

"What are you talking about?" Melissa demanded.

"I'm talking about this man you're keeping company with," Alberta declared.

The old Melissa would have slunk under the table. The new one just stared Alberta in the eye until the older woman looked away.

"What are you folks looking at?" Alberta demanded at the interested stares they were getting from the rest of the people eating under the tent's cover. "Go on and eat your food. This is a private conversation."

Melissa shared an amused look with Nick, who didn't look that fazed at having been called a jailbird.

"Sit down, Alberta, and tell me what all this nonsense is about," Melissa sternly ordered.

"I hate to be the one to tell you this, but this man has a record. He's one of those radical hippies."

"Nick was five years old in the age of radical hippies," Melissa calmly pointed out.

"I don't care what you call them, he's all for taking the law into his own hands. Going against authority."

"Do you have any idea what this is about?" Melissa asked Nick, who shook his head before taking another bite of bratwurst.

"Sure he'd deny it," Alberta scoffed. "What would you expect a criminal like him to do?"

"Watch who you're calling a criminal," Melissa warned Alberta with narrowed eyes.

Nick recognized that look—his champion Lissa.

"The man went to jail," Alberta stubbornly maintained. "He was found guilty and spent time in the slammer. I'll bet he didn't tell you that when he was slinging your lingerie around his lampshades!"

Nick glared at Alberta with such intensity that the older woman backed up. "You better not be saying anything against Melissa's reputation," he growled.

"You were the one who ruined her reputation by coming into the library the way you did," Alberta countered.

"My reputation is just fine," Melissa maintained, putting a restraining hand on Nick's tense arm.

"That's right," the entire table to Melissa's left shouted.

"Darn right," the table to her right seconded.

"So what are you talking about, Alberta?" Melissa demanded.

"Ask him," Alberta sniffed, pointing at Nick.

"I don't have a clue," he said with a shrug.

"I should have figured a man like you would lie. Well, fingerprints don't lie, Mr. Smarty-Pants. I had the sheriff trace your records from your fingerprints."

"What did she say?" ninety-year-old Mr. Obersdorf demanded, turning up his hearing aid. "Who's playing records? Don't shush me, girl," he rapped at his seventy-year-old daughter. "I'm missing something good here."

"We'll give you a written report later," Melissa mockingly promised Greely's oldest resident.

"See that you do. Don't leave out the good parts, neither," Mr. Obersdorf said. "Did you get them *Playboy* magazines in the library yet?"

"We're having a private conversation here, Silas," Alberta stiffly declared. "Butt out!"

"What was that about butts?" Mr. Obersdorf demanded.

Muttering under her breath, Melissa took hold of Alberta and dragged her outside. Once they were a safe distance from the tent, Melissa spoke. "I'm giving you one last chance, Alberta."

Alberta shoved a piece of paper at her. "It's all there. Read it for yourself."

Melissa did. Then she looked at Alberta in disbelief. "It says that Nick was arrested for being part of a demonstration against tearing down a historic building in Chicago."

Alberta nodded. "I told you he was one those civil disobedients."

"You've told me nothing," Melissa maintained, "except that Nick is even smarter than I gave him credit for."

"Why, thank you," Nick noted from her side, having just joined them.

"I support what Nick did. Heaven knows Chicago has enough parking lots. She's talking about your arrest in college," Melissa parenthetically told Nick. "When you protested that building being torn down."

"I'd almost forgotten about that," he reflected.

"The authorities haven't forgotten," Alberta declared.

"And this is why you called Nick a jailbird?" Melissa said in disbelief. "That's it?"

"It's enough." Alberta snatched the paper back and waved it under Melissa's nose. "He's got a record."

"One arrest for a civil disturbance does not make him a criminal. What happened to your theory that he was an impostor?"

"That didn't pan out yet," Alberta said. "But I'm not giving up."

"What would it take for you to believe me when I say I am Nick Grant?" Nick demanded. "The fact that Lissa and I were the ones who stole those apples off your back porch when you wanted to use them for the pie contest that summer?"

Alberta looked from Melissa to Nick, the incident clearly not forgotten even though it had taken place two decades ago. It was the one year Alberta *hadn't* won the blue ribbon at the country fair's pie contest. She'd thrown quite a fit, certain it had been an act of sabotage by her fellow competitors. "You two were the ones? Why, you thieving little—"

"Ah, ah, ah," Nick said with a warning shake of his finger.

"If he's not really Nick, how would he know that?" Melissa asked Alberta.

"Simple. The real Nick told him."

"I give up," Nick muttered.

Whereupon Melissa said, "Alberta, if it makes you happy to think Nick is someone else, then you go right ahead. But if I find out that you've made any more trouble, then I'll yank your library card." Of course, Melissa would never actually do such a thing, but Alberta didn't know that. "Are we clear?"

Nodding angrily, Alberta stalked off.

"I'm sorry about that," Melissa told Nick.

Reaching out to trail his index finger down her flushed cheek, he said, "I thought I was supposed to be the one saving you."

"Old habits die hard," she noted with a grin.

"Once a champion, always a champion, hmm?"

"Something like that, yes."

The warmth of feeling she experienced as her eyes met his was a familiar one. Their visual shorthand, a silent exchange straight from the heart, was as constant as her pulse. It spoke of times past and it held hidden promises of times to come.

The moment was cut short by the arrival of Beatrice. "I'm sorry I couldn't warn you about my sister," Beatrice said regretfully. "She didn't tell me what she was up to. And then I saw that nice Mr. Killian and I got distracted. I meant to keep an eye on Alberta, really, I did."

"Don't worry about it, Beatrice," Melissa said. "It's not your fault."

"Did she make an awful scene?"

"Actually, she was pretty good at it," Nick inserted.

He was rewarded by Beatrice's laughter.

Patting Melissa's hand, the older woman said, "Remember what I said about those rose leaves, Melissa. Unless you find you're no longer in doubt on the issue," she added with an air of meaningful anticipation.

"What issue?" Nick asked.

"Nothing," Melissa quickly replied. "We were having . . . a horticultural discussion."

"Right." He didn't sound at all convinced.

"You two—we need your help. We're short a couple in the three-legged race," Mrs. Cantrell breathlessly stated.

"Short a couple of what?" Beatrice asked in confusion.

"A couple. A man and a woman," Mrs. Cantrell clarified. "Come on, you two." She practically dragged Melissa and Nick over to the games area. "This is the last race and the last event I'm in charge of for the day. And then I'm never going to volunteer to be chairperson for the games and events ever again."

"You say that each year," someone good-naturedly shouted from the crowd.

"This year I mean it." The frazzled Mrs. Cantrell stuck a pencil in her graying hair and tried to check off the event on her clipboard with her glasses. "I'm getting too old for this," she muttered before switching pencil and glasses to their proper places. "What are you two waiting for?" she demanded of Nick and Melissa. "Take your places and get ready. Someone hand them some rags from the box there to use as ties. There now. You know the rules, Melissa. Your right leg tied to his left, above the knee and at the ankle. First couple across the finish line wins."

Melissa took the length of white material before hunkering down to tie her ankle to Nick's. He wore no socks, so her fingers brushed against his bare skin as she fastened the tie securely. Her fingertips tingled as she fumbled with the next tie, the one binding his thigh to hers. Since he was wearing cutoffs, once again she was touching the warmth of his skin, only this time more intimately. Her cheeks flushed as she bit her bottom lip and forced herself to concentrate on tying the knot.

"Need any help?" he inquired dryly.

She shook her head, which made her bangs fall in her eyes. Shoving them out of the way, she tried again, this time succeeding in getting the knot done right. Her skin tingled from ankle to thigh, heated by the warmth of his leg tied to hers. *Bound* to hers. The concept sank into her heart and lodged there with simple inevitability.

Taking a deep breath, she straightened, deliberately avoiding looking in Nick's eyes. Only then did she realize that Wayne and Rosie were in the race, as well. There were about a dozen couples lined up ready to start, which made Melissa wonder why Mrs. Cantrell felt she needed their presence.

As if hearing her thoughts, Mrs. Cantrell told Melissa, "It would be bad luck to have a race with thirteen couples." Turning to the group at large, she said, "Ready everyone?" At the many nods of agreement, she moved out of the runners' way. "Okay, on your mark, get set, go!"

After the trouble she'd had getting them ready, Melissa didn't expect the race to go well. But to her surprise she and Nick moved in perfect unison, racing neck-in-neck with their competitors. Nick had his arm around her waist, just as she had her arm around his. As couples awkwardly tangled and fell, she and Nick kept going, falling into a rhythm that ate up the distance between them and the finish line. Melissa was only vaguely aware of passing a stumbling Wayne and Rosie. The next thing she knew the crowd was cheering as she and Nick won the event.

Melissa threw her arms around Nick and hugged him, her laughing eyes shining at him with victorious triumph. "We did it!"

Holding her in his arms, Nick wanted time to stand still so this moment could be preserved forever. But he knew only too well how fleeting happiness like this could be. Melissa's exuberance was that of a friend, he sternly reminded himself as she leaned down to quickly undo the strips of material binding them together. He might have won the race, but he hadn't won her. Not yet.

Mrs. Cantrell was on hand to present Melissa and Nick with a pair of blue-ribbon pins stamped First Place. Melissa pinned hers on her pocket before turning to Nick and pinning his on his red T-shirt.

As she was doing so, Nick looked over her bent head to see Wayne looking at them with undisguised jealousy. Despite the fact that he was with Rosie, Wayne clearly couldn't keep his eyes off Melissa. Immersed in trying to fasten the pin onto Nick's chest, Melissa didn't notice her ex-fiancé's reaction.

But Nick did, and it reminded him of the bottom line here—that Melissa loved someone else. *Besides,* Nick reminded himself, *you're no prime catch yourself, a man who doesn't even know if he's capable of really loving someone.* Not that he had a lot of confidence in Wayne's capabilities in that department, either. But Nick *did* have confidence in Melissa's feelings. And she'd told him that she loved Wayne.

As for the passion Nick had shared with Melissa, he excused it as just physical chemistry on her part. Nick knew women found him attractive now. He knew Melissa thought so, too, and he figured that's why she'd responded to him when he'd kissed her. Then there was also the fact that she was on the rebound. The two taken together meant that she was vulnerable. Didn't take a rocket scientist to figure out that. It didn't mean she had any real feelings for him.

Nick's neatly tied together explanation didn't explain *his* feelings for Melissa, however. He wanted her, she loved someone else, he wanted her to be happy. God knew he was no expert in this field—this emotional mine field known as love. His own parents hadn't known what to make of him, had been disappointed in his early weaknesses.

Once, his dad had even claimed that Nick wasn't his son after all, that they must have been given the wrong baby at the hospital. At the time Nick had been eight and he'd actually hoped his father had been right. Because that would mean that it was okay that they didn't love him—because if he wasn't really their son, then *they* weren't really his parents. His *real* parents were out there somewhere, and they'd love him.

By the age of ten Nick had become more pragmatic about things, more accepting of fate. He wasn't fated to be loved or to love. He'd learned to accept it, just as he did math and Newton's laws of gravity.

Then he'd met Melissa that fateful summer when he'd turned eleven and things had changed. He'd gotten a taste of what it was like to have someone care for you, to have someone in your corner. It was a feeling he hungered for, and he'd eaten it up like someone who was starving.

But it had ended all too soon, in late August when he'd returned to his old life. Still, he'd held a flame inside, knowing that someone out there had found him worthy. When Nick's looks had changed, he'd once again been showered with attention. Only now he was cynical of the cause. Because he knew it was superficial—quickly given and just as quickly taken away. It wasn't real. Melissa was.

Which was why she deserved the best. And while Nick certainly didn't think Wayne came anywhere close to being the best, it wasn't his call to make. Wayne could make Melissa happy because she loved him. That was the bottom line.

So Nick would have to shelve his own emotions and do what was best for Melissa, even if it meant giving her up. He hated it. Despite what she might think, he was no good at noble acts of selfless benevolence and he was no knight in shining armor. A knight would have kept his distance. Nick hadn't. He was human. Just a man—more emotionally battered, more suspicious than most.

Wayne was the one used to winning. Nick was the one used to quietly going his own way. On his own.

You won today, Nick reminded himself, staring at the handmade first-place ribbon Melissa had just finished pinning on him. *And Melissa is with you, not with Wayne.*

Only because Wayne was taken. For the moment. Nick recognized the look in the other man's eyes. Wayne was having second thoughts, regrets about having let Melissa get away. Let her, hell—Wayne had *thrown* Melissa away. He didn't deserve a second chance. But if having the jerk would make her happy, Nick had to swallow his dismay and his pain and do whatever it took to make Melissa happy. Because she'd been the first person to ever believe in him.

Now Nick believed in *her,* and if nothing else, at least he'd shown her that she could be herself, that she was someone special. Her behavior today was evidence of his success in that direction. He had to be satisfied with that.

But one look at her sent all his self-directed words of wisdom flying out the proverbial window. As she stood in front of him, smiling that incredible smile of hers, her silky bangs falling into her eyes, Nick knew that he still wanted her, now more than ever. Was this his fate in life, then—to want what he couldn't have?

Melissa saw the brooding melancholy in his mysterious green eyes and wondered at its cause. "Is something wrong?" she asked. "You aren't having a good time? I mean, I realize this probably isn't the way you'd usually spend the holiday, running in a three-legged race."

"Usually I work through the holiday," he said.

"You know, I have a hard time seeing you in a suit and tie," Melissa confessed with a grin.

"It's not my attire of choice," Nick admitted.

"Not that you wouldn't look good in a suit and tie," she clarified.

"You think so? This wouldn't be your way of trying to get me into a suit and tie for that dance tonight, would it?"

"Good heavens, no. It's a square dance, not a formal affair at all. Which reminds me, I meant to ask if you'd mind if we met here at the park instead of you coming to my house. I've got to help Patty set up at the community center, so it would be easier if I could meet you here. In front of the building would be great."

"No problem. Sure you don't need any help setting up?"

"We can always use help. So just stop by whenever you're ready."

The problem was that Nick was ready now—ready to take Melissa in his arms, ready to kiss her, ready to make love to her. But he wasn't ready to do so at the cost of her happiness.

Melissa was outside the community center, taking a brief breather after completing her setup duties, when she saw Nick prowling through the crowd still gathered in the park in front of the building. Watching him, she was struck anew by the wonderful way he moved—swiftly, without hesitation, his bearing that of a man sure of who he was and what he was looking for—intent on one goal, one woman. Her.

She couldn't keep her eyes off him. He had a simply incredible walk—part saunter, pure poetry, with just a touch of swagger. No, not swagger, she immediately corrected herself. That denoted arrogance rather than confidence. Nick wasn't arrogant. Shoulders thrown back, he carried himself like a nobleman. Or a knight.

And then he saw her. Even though he was several feet away, she felt his gaze as if he was right beside her. The surrounding crowd faded into the background as Nick came closer, his gaze never leaving hers. Taking her hand in his, he tugged her after him—away from the doorway and the heavy traffic in front of the building. She went willingly, still caught up in the magic of his approach.

Ducking beneath the huge willow behind the community center, he let the fronds return to the ground, effectively screening them from the outside in a world of verdant enchantment. Through the thin material of her gingham dress, Melissa felt the roughness of the bark on the willow's trunk at her back. Bracing one hand above her head, Nick leaned closer to trail his fingertips over her skin, as lightly as the willow branches trailed over the grass in the soft breeze.

"You look beautiful," he said softly. His voice was as magical as his walk was, she dreamily decided. He spoke softly, yet more powerfully than a shout, thanks to the commanding wealth of his expressive voice. It rolled over her like warm syrup.

"You look nice, too," she shyly replied, her hands hovering over the whiteness of his shirt as if she longed to touch him but knew she shouldn't.

Nick knew he shouldn't be tempting her, shouldn't be tempting himself. But he couldn't resist.

In the shadowy confines of the willow's haven, Melissa saw the hunger in his eyes—eyes that were as green as the willow's leaves and as mysterious as all mankind.

Her gaze lowered to his white shirt, the one she was fingering. She recognized it as the one she'd worn after her shower at his cabin. The one she'd discarded in front of the fireplace. Or was she imagining things? Nick probably owned several white shirts. There was no reason to think this was the same one. But she did.

Her gaze returned to his eyes, as if hoping to read the answer there. Instead, she saw more questions.

"Melissa, are you out here?" The sound of Mrs. Cantrell's voice pierced their retreat. "The mayor is looking for you."

"We'd better go," Melissa said regretfully.

Nick nodded. When she lowered her arms to her sides and looked away, her hair slid over her cheek, shielding her face from view. Nick gently gathered the silky strands and hooked them behind her ear. His smile was as powerful as a kiss and left Melissa about as breathless.

When they entered the community center, the place was already crowded. "Oh, there you are," Mrs. Cantrell said in relief. "The mayor was looking for you."

A second later the mayor joined them. "We got almost a thousand dollars for the library's fund today," he triumphantly announced.

"That's wonderful!" Melissa exclaimed.

"Worth celebrating, I'd say," the mayor stated, handing her a paper cup filled with punch. Seeing Nick at her side, the mayor grabbed another paper cup from the table behind him.

"Thanks," Nick said.

"Name's Tom Trout," the mayor said jovially. "What's yours?"

"Nick Grant."

"Welcome to Greely, Nick," the mayor said with the hearty handshake of a politician. "This your first time here?"

"No. I visited here once when I was a kid."

"Bet you didn't find the place much changed, huh?" the mayor asked.

"Some things changed," Nick noted, his eyes on Melissa. "Some things improved. Some are better than I remembered."

"That's what we like to hear," the mayor said. "Well, let me propose a toast. First to the successful day's takings for the library."

Melissa lifted her paper cup for the toast. After taking a sip, the mayor proposed another toast. "And a warm welcome to our newest visitor to Greely. May he continue to find much here to hold his interest."

"I'm sure I will," Nick agreed with a lift of his cup.

"Now then, Nick, are you and Melissa going to join us for some square dancing?"

"No, sir. Dancing isn't my thing."

"I wouldn't say that," Melissa whispered with a grin, remembering his smooth moves to the classic rock music blaring from the clock radio at his cabin.

"*Square* dancing isn't my thing," Nick clarified.

"Well, then, Melissa, I guess it's just you and me," the mayor announced.

"Oh, no, I can't...."

"Sure you can," the mayor heartily stated. "This first dance is specifically for beginners. All of us old-timers are duty-bound to dance with beginners and teach them some of the steps. Just listen to the caller," he added as he tugged Melissa onto the dance floor, where other couples were setting up in the square configurations that gave the dancing its name.

There were eight people, four couples to a set. That much Melissa knew from years gone past—years when she'd managed to avoid getting roped in to dancing. She'd done enough square dancing in third grade to know it wasn't her favorite activity.

She cast a frantic look in Nick's direction only to find Peggy Sue homing in on him with the speed of a heat-seeking missile. In the blink of an eye, the woman was batting her false eyelashes at him while Melissa pretended to listen to the mayor's instructions on the upcoming steps.

The caller came to the microphone as the unconventional band—a bass fiddler, a guitarist, an accordion player and a banjo player—started in on a hoedown classic. Melissa heard the familiar opening:

"All square your sets around the hall.
   Four couples to a set, listen to the call."

She found it hard to concentrate on what she was doing when her thoughts were on Nick. Her eyes, as well.

"All hands join, circle left you know.
   All the way around and don't be slow."

No one could accuse Peggy Sue of being slow, Melissa angrily noted as she moved in a circle with the others. The woman was hanging all over Nick.

"All face your partners, do a do-si-do
   Go all around your own just so."

Nick was *her* own, not Peggy Sue's! The thought hit Melissa as abruptly as running into the mayor did.

"You gotta pay attention, girl," he chastised her.

Melissa breathlessly tried to comply, but found it hard to keep up when she kept looking for Nick over her shoulder and consequently bumping into the other couples. Thankfully the beginners' set was a brief one—a repeat of the second and third call, and then the finish.

"Make your move, gents of Greely
   But take care, don't get feely!"

That refrain was the caller's way of saying that the square dancing was done and the slow dancing was about to begin.

Breathlessly making her apologies and excuses, Melissa left the floor, went over to Nick and held out her hand. Her heart swelled at the speed with which he accepted her unspoken invitation, leaving a peeved Peggy Sue behind.

As Melissa and Nick walked onto the dance floor, she remembered all too well the last time they'd danced together, with wanton abandon in front of the fireplace. As if they were the only two people on the face of the earth. In a way, Melissa felt like that again, even though they were surrounded by people. With her hand in his—palm pressed to palm, fingers intertwined—the magic flowed.

The band started playing a Paul Anka tune from the fifties, "Put Your Head on My Shoulder." Melissa did, obeying the song's lyrics and her own desires, and noticing anew how well placed Nick's shoulder was for this purpose. He wasn't so tall that she had to stand on her tiptoes in order to dance comfortably with him, nor so short that they looked eye to eye.

Instead, when she stood in front of him, his lips hit the middle of her forehead. She knew because his breath stirred her bangs. And when she leaned forward, as she was doing now, her head came to rest naturally on the reassuring solidity of his shoulder.

His two-step was a light, gliding slide that matched the smoothness of his other moves. Closing her eyes, Melissa let herself be swept away by the moment, all thoughts of Wayne erased from her mind. And so it remained throughout the next three slow songs.

When the band finally took a break, Nick got more punch for both of them. The next thing Melissa knew, Rosie was standing next to her, outwardly smiling although her tone of voice was anything but friendly.

"Your little plan isn't going to work," Rosie informed her in a furious undertone. "I know what you're up to. You want Wayne back and you think you can make him jealous. It won't work," she desperately declared. "He's mine now, and you can't have him!"

Startled by Rosie's verbal attack, Melissa didn't know what to say, so she said nothing, which only seemed to infuriate Rosie even more.

"You think you're so clever, don't you? Dragging this man back here and throwing him in Wayne's face. It's not as if anyone else has been interested in you for years."

"I tend to be more discriminating than you, Rosie," Melissa retorted. "And I don't intend to stand here and get into a cat fight with you. Excuse me." Head held high, Melissa walked away.

"There's someone outside who wants to talk to you," a stranger told Nick, who was standing in the long line at the punch bowl.

Turning to look for Melissa, Nick couldn't see her in the crowd. She must be the one outside waiting for him. Abandoning the line, he threaded his way through the crush and headed for the entrance.

Outside, the air was sultry with humidity. A small group was gathered off to one side, beneath a wide-spread oak tree. Noting that they didn't grow trees that way in Chicago, Nick headed for the group, searching for Melissa.

He neared the fringe of the group when he heard one of the members growl his name. "Nick Grant, we don't need your kind around here!"

A second later Nick saw a punch come flying straight at him!

Melissa finally made her way outside after having been stopped by what felt like half of Greely on her way out. She needed some time to herself after Rosie's confrontation. The hot air outside hit her like a fist—and so did the sight of Nick ducking a punch! Someone was trying to hit him!

The drunken cheers of a small group of men seemed to be encouraging the man—Melissa couldn't make out who it was—in his fight with Nick. She was all set to fly down the steps and come to Nick's aid when she saw him move in a blur of motion. A second later Nick's attacker was on the ground. In an instant the man's drunken buddies scattered like grass seeds in the wind.

"What's going on out here?" Melissa heard the booming voice of Sheriff Edelman demand as he stepped into the fray.

Only Nick, his attacker and one other man who had his back to her remained for the sheriff to question.

"I asked you a question, boy," the sheriff told Nick, his inflection hostile. "We don't take well to this kind of behavior around here."

Melissa stood frozen, unable to comprehend the violence she'd just witnessed. Why would anyone want to hurt Nick?

"I was told there was someone out here who wanted to talk to me," Nick began.

"So you came out here and started a fight."

"No." Nick's voice was cool but calm. "The other guy threw the first punch. I was just protecting myself."

The sheriff turned to Nick's attacker, who sat on the ground, nursing his injuries. "That what happened, Johnny?"

"Hell, no," Johnny denied. "I was talking with my buddies when this guy came at me."

"Why would I attack you?" Nick reasonably asked. "I don't even know you."

Melissa knew him. Johnny Givens was a rabble-rouser. And he was Peggy Sue's latest conquest. She kept picking them younger and younger—and wilder and wilder.

Johnny groaned instead of answering Nick's question, playing up his injury for all it was worth.

"I think we better finish this conversation down at the station," the sheriff declared. "Come on, both of you."

"Wait a second. Wayne saw what happened," Nick curtly stated.

"That so, Wayne?" the sheriff asked.

"I really couldn't see what happened," Wayne replied with just a hint of gloating complacency. "I couldn't say what was going on."

"That's okay, because I *can* say what went on," Melissa announced as she joined the men. "And it stinks!" This time her comment was directed to Wayne, who paled when he saw her. Turning to the sheriff, she said, "I was standing by the building and I saw the entire thing. Johnny threw the first punch."

"How do you know that?" Sheriff Edelman demanded.

"I saw him."

Frowning, the sheriff continued his interrogation. "How long had you been outside when you saw that?"

"I'd just come out."

"Ah, so you could have missed Nick attacking Johnny and just seen Johnny protecting himself."

"No," Melissa stated with pugnacious certainty.

"Then how can you be sure what happened?"

"Because I know Nick. And you know Johnny, Sheriff. You should, you've seen him often enough."

The sheriff shifted uncomfortably, turning to Wayne as if seeking guidance. Melissa knew all too well how much of a football fan the sheriff was and how highly he held Wayne in his esteem—highly enough to be willing to take part in a scam like this for him.

Melissa directed her fury at her former fiancé. "I can't believe you tried to pull something like this! What, you couldn't take the fact that Nick and I beat you in that three-legged race? Or is this your childish way of getting back at me for dunking you at the fair today?"

"I'm not the one who's being childish, you are," Wayne countered angrily. "Flaunting this guy in my face."

"So you set up an incident to get Nick in trouble. That's real mature."

"I did no such thing," Wayne protested.

"I hit the guy on my own," Johnny inserted. "No one has to tell me what to do. When Wayne told me that this Nick Grant guy was hitting on Peggy Sue, I knew what I had to do."

"There you have it, Sheriff. A confession," Melissa said.

"From a drunken man," Sheriff Edelman countered.

"And a known troublemaker," Melissa shot right back.

The sheriff was quiet a moment as he considered his options, his gaze returning to Wayne. Then as if reaching a decision, he slowly pulled Johnny to his feet. "I think I better take you with me down to the station just to make sure you sober up." Turning to Nick, Sheriff Edelman very reluctantly asked, "Do you intend to press any charges as a result of this incident?"

Nick shook his head. "I can see how this misunderstanding got started," he said, his voice quiet but dangerous nonetheless as he stared directly at Wayne.

"I can see, too," Melissa seconded.

His face turning red—with anger or with guilt, Melissa couldn't be sure—Wayne stalked off.

Turning to face her, Nick mockingly murmured, "I thought you said the fireworks didn't start until after dark?"

* * *

"Are you sure you're all right?" Melissa asked for what had to be the dozenth time since they'd reached their chosen viewing place for the fireworks display. Nick had creatively suggested the lake. Since the land around Greely was as flat as a pancake, they'd be able to get a great view, with the fireworks reflecting in the lake's mirroring darkness.

"I'm fine," Nick assured her. "Stop wiggling. You're rocking the boat."

"Hell-raisers tend to do that a lot," she retorted. They were in the rowboat, the one they'd taken out during the storm. Tonight the skies were clear, and the stars shimmered.

"I didn't say you were a hell-raiser," Nick corrected her. "I said you were hell on wheels. Not the same thing. Quite." His smile was slow and infinitely appealing.

Melissa reached out to touch his jaw. "I'm glad he didn't hurt you. I'm sorry it happened."

"I'm not," Nick replied softly, pressing her hand to his cheek before kissing it. How could he tell her that it would have been worth getting punched ten times to have her look at him like this?

"Where did you learn that...whatever it is you did to protect yourself?"

"It's called *T'ai Chi Ch'üan*, and it's a Taoist martial art."

"I've never heard of it."

"The basic idea is to wear your opponent out either by sending his energy back at him or by deflecting it, keeping him off-balance."

Melissa knew from personal experience that Nick was an expert at keeping *her* off-balance.

"Other people might fight fire with fire, but I prefer to fight fire with water," Nick said.

He didn't always do that, Melissa silently noted, her smile dreamy as she remembered their shared passion in front of the fireplace . . . when he'd met the fire of her passion with an ardent fire of his own.

Her sensual memories were interrupted by a star burst of liquid light in the night sky. The fireworks display was starting. Nick had the rowboat positioned in such a way that Melissa would get a crick in her neck unless she joined him where he sat on the bottom of the boat's shell, facing the prow, his back against the wooden seat. He'd created a comfortable nest among the life vests. There wasn't enough room to stretch out beside him, so she had to settle in the open V of his legs, resting against his chest. Putting his arms around her waist, he rubbed his chin over the top of her head.

Lying so close to him, Melissa could feel the attraction growing with every breath she took. Like the fireworks show, her relationship with Nick had started out with smaller explosions before increasing the pace to the spectacular grand finale. As the fireworks show drew to an end, Melissa knew that the time had come for their own grand finale.

When Nick rowed to the dock, Melissa readily accepted his offer of a cool drink. Instead of waiting out on the porch, she entered the cabin with him. It was too hot to start a fire tonight—at least in the fireplace, she silently noted with a grin.

The pillows were still strewn in front of the fireplace, as they had been the last time they'd come in from the lake. Only this time Melissa knew what she wanted, knew what would make her happy. Sinking down onto the pillows, she waited until Nick turned from his review of the antique refrigerator's contents.

Looking at her over the top of the open ice-box door, he said, "I've got root beer, or beer." He held both cans up for her perusal. "What do you think?"

Slowly unbuttoning the top three buttons on her dress, Melissa offered herself up for his perusal as she huskily replied, "I think it's time we finished what we started."

Nine

"What are you doing?" Nick's voice was stunned as he made a last-minute effort to save the icy cans in his hands from crashing to the floor.

"What does it look like I'm doing?" Melissa asked, undoing another two buttons.

"Wait!" Nick rushed over and put a hand over hers, effectively halting her in her proverbial tracks.

Had she misunderstood him? Didn't he want her, after all? Her face flamed with embarrassment as he suddenly snatched his hand away as if scalded.

"You don't have to do this, Melissa."

His voice sounded strangled. Probably with embarrassment, she told herself, tears threatening to overwhelm her. "I'm sorry," she mumbled, her head lowered so that her hair shielded her face as she unsteadily attempted to close the self-covered buttons she'd undone. "I must have misunderstood...." Her throat closed, the self-control damming her tears about to break wide open. She had to get out of here, and fast. She leapt to her feet, but Nick held on to her hand.

"It's not that I don't want to," he huskily assured her, his fingers sliding over her face as if irresistibly drawn by a magnetic force.

"Then what?" she whispered.

"You're on the rebound from a broken engagement." The words sounded torn from him.

"Patty thinks I should say I'm going through a relationship adjustment," Melissa said with an unsteady smile and the slightest of sniffs.

Nick wiped away the single tear that spilled over and slipped down her cheek. "You're not ready for this."

"Aren't I, Nick?" she challenged him. "Feel the pounding of my heart." Taking his right hand, she placed it on her left breast. Her fingertips rested on the pulse on his wrist, and she felt the rapid beat of his heart. It mirrored her own.

"You're not thinking clearly," he said with more than a tinge of desperation.

Melissa's confidence was making a gradual comeback. She could see the look in his eyes. It was the look of a man trying to do the right thing when he badly wanted to do the opposite.

"I'm thinking very clearly," she maintained, her tongue darting out to lick her lips.

Nick's gaze fastened on her mouth. "What about Wayne?" he asked in a raspy voice.

"That's over."

"How can you be sure?"

"This way..." Leaning forward, she kissed him. It was the first time she'd ever taken the initiative, and she cursed herself for not doing so earlier. For this was a man who was confident enough to meet her halfway—who wanted her for who she was, as wild as she wanted, as free as she desired.

Her kiss reflected her feelings, saying what she couldn't. It came from her heart, and he answered in the same way— wholeheartedly, no holds barred, with nothing left to hide. There was no teasing prelude, no feathery dalliance. Instead, there was an urgent sense of hunger as his mouth slanted ravenously over hers.

Fire licked her, submerging her in a sea of flames as he dipped his tongue into the warm depths of her mouth. Melissa responded by sliding her arms around his neck, holding on to him for dear life as her knees threatened to give way. The fireworks they'd just watched over the lake were nothing compared to the ones going off inside her, spiraling Catherine wheels of pleasure. Just from a kiss.

When he cupped her breast in his palm, the excitement sparked a new level of intensity. His hands joined in the seduction, remembering every curve as if he'd touched her only seconds before—brushing his thumb over her nipple, murmuring his pleasure at her response. Melissa was awed that she could feel such joy while there were still two layers of material between his skin and hers. It made her yearn for those barriers to be gone, enabling her to feel the full force of him touching her.

Seconds later, his right hand shifted to trail behind her ear, sliding down her throat, tipping up her chin to change the angle of their next kiss before tracing a path of fire from the hollow of her collarbone down to the scooped neckline of her dress. Once there, he rapidly undid the remaining buttons before attacking the front fastening of her bra with muttered complaints about the complicated intricacies of feminine attire.

Loath to give up her examination of him, Melissa sent one hand to assist his, their fingers tangling as were their tongues. Once their mission was finally accomplished, Nick broke off their searing kiss to bury his lips in the newly revealed valley between her breasts. Melissa slid her fingers through his hair as she gasped at the delight of his tongue stroking her bare skin.

A second later, he scooped her up in his arms and carried her into the bedroom.

Carefully laying her on the bedspread, he said once again, "Are you sure?"

"I'm positive," she murmured.

No more words were spoken after that, verbal communication being abandoned in favor of a more direct means of communication as ageless as time itself. Instead of peeling her dress over her head, Nick unbuttoned every button clear down to the hem, peeling it back as if unwrapping the most revered of treasures. Melissa protested at the way her arms were pinned at her side, preventing her from reaching out and touching him as he was touching her.

Murmuring something about patience, Nick mapped every inch of her creamy skin with his mouth—varying his technique as he alternately skimmed, nibbled, licked his way from her throat to her navel and lower.

Shivering with anticipation, Melissa felt as if she were about to burst into flames. Lifting his head, Nick looked down at her. God, what he could promise with those eyes! They stared at her with green fire, radiating heat as surely as his body was. The dark promises of his eyes were being enacted by his skillful hands, as they slid up her bare leg, stroking the back of her knee before moving upward to the inner curve of her thigh, tracing imaginary circles that came closer and closer to the part of her that was aching to be touched.

Passion radiated from every portion of his body as he lowered his head to kiss her—darkly, intimately—his tongue delving into the darkness of her mouth even as his fingers delved beneath the elastic of her panties to caress her there before dipping into her moist warmth. The thrust of his tongue mimicked the motion of his finger, moving in and out, swirling and curving.

Melissa grabbed handfuls of the bedspread as elation pooled deep within her, spiraling and tightening with every creative movement of his hand—growing, growing until it suddenly crescendoed into hard-edged waves of ecstasy.

Lifting his head, he watched her, his eyes dark with passion as she shuddered in climax. The stunned look on her face aroused him more than he thought possible. Regretfully moving his hand, he knew he had to slow things down or he'd explode.

But Melissa had other ideas. Hooking her leg around his, she rolled over so that she was perched on top of him. Nick groaned as she settled over the crotch of his jeans, her hands propped on his shoulders. Impatiently lifting her arms, she rapidly got rid of her dress, letting it fall to the floor. Her bra followed. With no light but the moonlight coming in through the window, she undid the buttons on his shirt with slow precision, making sure to shift against his lower torso every second or so.

The ensuing friction was as arousing to her as it was to him. She could feel his throbbing hardness straining against the confines of his jeans. Now that his shirt was undone, she opened it the same way he'd opened her dress, trapping his arms in his shirtsleeves. Leaning forward, she licked her way from his collarbone to his navel, grinning as he bucked against her in an instinctive move.

Murmuring something about patience, she sat up and directed her attention toward the taut fastening of his jeans, brushing her hands against him with a seductive show of feminine wiles, undoing the top button with her fingers before leaning down and delicately grasping the zipper pull in her teeth and lowering it ever so slowly.

"That does it," Nick growled, dislodging her to rip off his clothes himself. Removing her panties with one hand, he used the other to reach into the bedside table drawer and grab the plastic packet stored there, smacking it into Melissa's hand. "You started this, now you can finish it," he murmured.

Melissa cracked up. Not the response he was looking for.

Looking at her hand, he saw the reason for her amusement. He'd just handed her a packet of aspirin. "See what you do to me?" he said. "I can't even think straight anymore."

"I love *seeing* what I do to you," she assured him with a saucy grin, reaching out to cup him in her hand. "Seeing and feeling . . ."

Muttering darkly, he reached into the drawer again, this time coming up with the condom he'd been looking for and slapping it into her free hand with fingers that shook. She sheathed him with the latex condom moments before sheathing him with her body as he came to her in one smooth surge.

Cupping her face with his hands, he lovingly kissed her. Melissa clasped him to her, passionately absorbing the weight of him, the feel of him moving deep within her. Every sliding surge stroked the flames of her earlier completion, resetting the fire and promising to make it burn out of control.

Her breath caught as she felt it again, the growing pulses of bliss, enlarging and expanding, propelling her onward . . . upward . . . before bursting free in an explosion of joy. Crying out his name, she clung to him, the only solid thing in a world whirling wildly—blissful wave after wave washing over her.

Moments later he stiffened as he, too, reached his climax before collapsing in her arms.

Melissa was the first to speak. "You remember talking about fighting fire with water?" she murmured lazily. "I think you just proved that fighting fire with *waves* is the most incredible experience on the face of this earth."

Their legs were still intertwined as they lay in satiated abandon on top of the bed.

Nick smiled, a slow, sultry smile. "You're gonna give me a swollen head."

"Something is definitely showing signs of life," she noted seductively, bending her knee and running her calf over his. Resting on his chest the way she was, she could feel his heart pounding beneath her hand.

"How many more…aspirin do you have in that drawer?" she inquired, her smile a study of wicked innocence.

"A box full," he replied, dislodging her long enough to prove his claim, sliding them out of the box in an abundant display.

Another thought abruptly hit her. "Tell me you didn't buy these at Radizchek's drugstore in town."

"I didn't buy these at Radizchek's drugstore," he obediently told her. "I bet they don't even sell them there."

"They sell everything there, from aspirin to zippers."

"Zippers, hmm?" he noted, his voice a velvety rumble in her ear. "That reminds me…."

He shifted until they were both on their sides, nose to nose, chest to chest, hardness to softness. Sliding his hand beneath her knee, he hooked her leg around him. Rubbing his nose against her, he grinned at her wide-eyed look of appreciation as another part of his anatomy rubbed against her, as well.

"Looks like it's time for another...aspirin, huh?" he noted wickedly.

The moment that was accomplished, he came to her again, once more taking her to that free-fall of ecstasy before joining her in the vortex of passion.

Nick awoke the next morning to the smell of honeysuckle wafting through his window. Only this morning the honeysuckle smelled particularly sweet. Shifting, he realized that was because he had his nose buried in the silky softness of Melissa's hair as she lay spoon fashion, curved against him, still asleep.

Nick had fallen for Melissa some time ago. He couldn't even remember when it had happened. From their first kiss, designed to throw the Beasley sisters off track? Or had it been from the moment she'd clobbered him with that blueberry pie? He no longer knew.

He only knew that he loved her. He'd never felt this way before. He loved everything about her, her courage in the face of adversity, her spirit, her humor, her silky, sweet-smelling hair, the way she curled her bare toes when she was happy, her smile, her loyalty.

His smile faded. While he knew he loved her, he still didn't know how she felt about him. Despite the fact that she went to bed with him, she hadn't said she loved him. He knew she'd said she was over Wayne, but he also knew that she was still struggling to come to terms with her emotions.

Nick realized that in the past the women in his life had been drawn by his good looks and repelled by his inability to love, his loner ways. He'd always been a loner...except with Melissa. Why had it taken him so long to see that? And what would have happened had he not returned to Greely and met her again?

He didn't want to think what life would be like without
her. Darkness without sunshine. He tenderly smoothed her
bangs away from her eyes. He wanted to marry her. He
wanted to spend the rest of his life with her, grow old with
her.

But what did Melissa want? For him to make her forget
Wayne?

Nick stared at her face as if trying to see into her mind or
her heart. She had to love him. She just didn't know it yet.
But he was definitely going to show her, convince her that
he was the only man for her. "Prepare yourself, Melissa
Carlson," he murmured purposefully. "You're about to be
courted."

"Concentrate, Melissa," she ordered herself as she tried
for the fourth time to tally the previous month's library circulation records on a calculator. So far she'd come up with
a different total every time. Clearly her mind was not on her
work.

Her mind was on Nick and the incredible night they'd
shared last night. Hitting the clear button, she entered the
numbers again. Greely's library was scheduled to get a
computerized circulation system soon, but they told her that
each year. And each year the funds weren't yet available. So
it was still the old-fashioned method for her.

Nick was old-fashioned, too, in some ways. And incredibly advanced in others. Her smile turned dreamy again.
There were still some things she wasn't sure of, but she *was*
sure she'd done the right thing in making love with Nick.
She'd woken this morning with no regrets. Getting to her
own house without anyone seeing her had been a bit tricky,
but they hadn't encountered anyone in the two blocks. Of
course it had been barely dawn.

At her insistence, Nick had only walked halfway with her. While her neighbors to the south were on vacation in California and the house to the north was vacant and for sale, Melissa hadn't wanted to risk someone seeing her in the same dress she'd worn last night. She and Nick would have to be discreet. There had been nothing discreet about her behavior with him last night, however. She'd been wild and free. She'd never dreamed of doing anything like that with Wayne.

There was simply no comparison. She'd had no idea what she was missing until Nick had shown her last night. She'd simply assumed the physical aspects of a relationship had been somewhat overrated. Now she knew better.

Looking down at the calculator, she saw that the total number of books checked out last month was over ten million. Amazing, since the library only had twenty-some thousand books in the entire collection! Muttering under her breath, she hit the clear button yet again.

This time she got it right. A little under six hundred transactions. That was par for the course. Summers were slow periods for the library. Things picked up in the fall, when the kids were back in school. Then Melissa got additional help from several students who worked at the library through the work-study program at the high school.

Once her paperwork was done, she launched into a more creative project—changing the display case near the front door from its red-white-and-blue Independence Day theme to a reminder about the upcoming book drive. The sale of donated books not used for the collection brought in a sizable amount each year.

She finished in time for her lunch hour, which she'd planned to spend with Patty. Nick had wanted to spend time with her, but Melissa had a commitment to Patty and she wasn't prepared to break it—she needed to talk to her best friend about this latest development in her "relationship adjustments."

After turning the sign on the library door to read Closed, the two women picked up a couple of burgers and some fries from the closest fast-food outlet and then headed for the privacy of Melissa's house. Melissa didn't want anyone overhearing their girl talk.

"So come on, you've been bursting to tell me something," Patty said the second they entered Melissa's house. "What gives?"

"I did. Last night. With Nick." Melissa echoed Patty's excited shriek. "I know. I can't believe I just spit it out like that!"

"That's what friends are for," Patty assured her with a grin before munching on a perfectly done fry. "To spill your guts to. So go ahead. Tell me all the delicious details."

Melissa looked at her. Patty wiggled her eyebrows at Melissa, and seconds later the two of them cracked up into gales of laughter, just as they had as teenagers. Patty's mom had often found them rolling on the floor, laughing over something only they understood. She'd just walk away, shaking her head over their antics.

Gripping her sore stomach muscles with one hand, Melissa wiped away the tears of mirth with the other. "This is ridiculous," she managed to get out. "I don't even know what we're laughing about. Do you?"

Patty shook her head and tried to compose her features, but only managed to set Melissa off again.

It took a minute or two for them to regain their composure. "It felt good to laugh like that again," Patty noted nostalgically.

Melissa nodded. "Yeah, it did."

"It's been a long time."

Melissa nodded again.

"I like your Nick," Patty said.

"I like him, too," Melissa murmured.

"I'd say you more than like him, Melissa," she dryly observed.

"He's not *my* Nick," Melissa belatedly corrected Patty.

"Why not?"

"I'm not sure where this relationship with Nick is going."

"Where do you want it to go?"

"I'm not sure. It's so soon after Wayne."

"So what made you decide to move forward with Nick? There wasn't time for you to take Beatrice's advice with the rosebush leaves," she added in a teasing voice.

"It was a combination of things," Melissa noted. "And it didn't just happen yesterday. A lot of things led up to my being with Nick. But there were a few turning points for me. The main one was seeing Wayne in a different light."

"With Rosie, you mean?"

"Not at all. That didn't really bother me. To tell you the truth, I wasn't even paying that much attention to them. Which tells you something right there. No, I meant the incident with Wayne and the sheriff."

"Wait a second! I don't know anything about this."

"At Wayne's instigation, Johnny Givens tried to punch Nick last night." Seeing Patty's shocked and confused look, Melissa added, "Johnny has been seeing Peggy Sue, and Wayne made a point of telling an inebriated Johnny that Nick was hitting on Peggy Sue, which of course Nick wasn't. Quite the opposite, in fact. Peggy Sue was drooling all over Nick!"

"And Johnny got jealous. So he started a fight with Nick," Patty ventured.

Melissa nodded. "I saw what happened. So did Wayne. But when the sheriff just happened to conveniently show up,

Wayne claimed he hadn't seen a thing, and Johnny said that
Nick was the one who'd started the fight. Sheriff Edelman
was all set to take *both* Nick and Johnny down to the station when I stepped in. I'd seen what happened. I know that
Wayne did, too. He was just trying to get Nick into trouble."

"Because Wayne was jealous of Nick," Patty stated.

Melissa nodded.

"You know Wayne hates to lose," Patty pointed out. "At
anything. He's very competitive. I actually heard him tell
someone that he let you and Nick win that race yesterday."

Their conversation was interrupted by the arrival of
Magic, who had just gotten a whiff of the hamburgers from
her resting place upstairs on Melissa's bed. The cat came
racing into the room as if jet-propelled, hit a rag rug in the
hallway as she made a turn and slid with it several feet before hanging a sharp right, narrowly missing the door-
frame and tearing into the living room.

"I read that they've clocked house cats going at something like thirty miles a minute," Patty noted with a grin.
"Don't know if it's true or not."

"Wouldn't surprise me." Melissa tore off a piece of her
hamburger and put it on the paper bag before lowering it to
the floor. The cat gobbled the piece of meat and looked up
for more, the expression on her face clearly saying, *Okay,
that was a nice appetizer. Where's the main course?*

Melissa dropped a few more pieces and added a small slice
of pickle.

"She likes pickles," Melissa explained.

The food was gone an instant later.

Patty added her contribution to Magic's culinary cause,
saying, "If she likes pickles, maybe she'll like the hamburger bun, too. It probably smells like hamburger, and

since she can't see very well, she won't know the difference.''

"Sure, she will," Melissa noted. "Watch."

The cat again inhaled the meat but merely sniffed at the hamburger bun before lifting her feline head to give them both a look. *What, do you think I'm stupid?* She left the bun and moved a few feet away to begin daintily licking her paw and running it over her face from ears to whiskers.

"You've got it good," Patty told Magic, who paused to look at her before resuming her grooming duties.

"She's got it good, and I've got it bad," Melissa noted wryly. "It was all I could do to keep my mind on work this morning. I kept thinking of Nick."

"I hope things work out," Patty said. "You deserve to be happy."

Did she? Sometimes, Melissa wondered.

"Cherries in the Snow... what kind of name is that for nail polish, anyway?" Nick asked as he sat on the foot of Melissa's bed. They'd spent the evening together—having dinner, watching ten minutes of a video before coming upstairs to make love. And it wasn't even ten yet.

Nick had brought up a plate with a healthy slice of blueberry pie on it while Melissa—fresh out of the shower—had been doing her toenails, trying to hurry.

Blushing at getting caught, she'd swiftly put the lid on the fast-drying nail polish. But she already had four of her ten toes painted. Nick had handed her the plate and taken over the job himself, reminding her that he'd been rather good at painting as a kid.

He was wearing a navy silk robe, one she'd foolishly gotten for her father last Christmas only to have him return it to her with a curt note saying he never wore "stuff" like that.

Now she was glad he'd returned it, because Nick looked great in it. He was leaning back against the bed's white enamel footboard, and he had her bare foot propped against his lower chest, where he was carefully brushing polish over her toenails. His fingers were warm as he circled her ankle with one hand to hold her foot still. "How is your scar doing from that sliver you got in your foot a few weeks ago?"

"It's healed fine. I won't be marked for life," she said teasingly.

"Unlike me."

"What are you talking about?"

"This." Putting the brush in the small bottle, he held up his left thumb for her perusal.

Bending her leg, she scooted closer to get a better look.

"A permanent memory of the time we became blood brothers. You sliced us both open with a steak knife the day before I left," he reminded her. "The wound got infected and I was left with a scar."

She looked at him, her eyes reflecting her remorse. "I'm so sorry."

"I'm not. Many a time I've looked down at that scar over the years and gained strength from it."

Leaning forward, she kissed the small injury. Seeing the darkening fire in his green eyes, she quickly scooted back to her original position. "You're not done yet," she said.

"You've got that right," he agreed with a slow smile. "I'm just getting started." He completed the final brush strokes to her baby toe.

"It's fast-drying nail polish," she told him, her voice breathless from laughter and budding excitement.

"Stop laughing," he scolded her as he set the polish aside. "You're going to ruin all my good work." Lifting her right foot higher, he studied his handiwork, and the bare length of her leg. Since she was only wearing a sheet, his view was an intimate one.

"Stop that!" She almost upended the plate of pie in the process of smoothing the sheet over her lower torso. "I had no idea you'd grow up to be a devious man with a foot fetish," she wickedly teased him.

Nick made no reply, although his smile spoke volumes— all of them X-rated. He slid his long fingers between her toes before shifting his attention, and his caresses, to the curve of her instep. Melissa shivered at the delicious feel of his creative touch exploring her foot as if he were Columbus and she the New World.

He soon expanded his sensual survey, his adventuring hands sliding up her leg to the back of her knee. And all the while he was inching her closer to him, using his hold on her leg to bring her nearer to the foot of the bed. The back of her knee proved to be extremely vulnerable to his swirling touch. His lifting her leg to kiss the back of her knee resulted in her being forced onto her back as he upended her— literally and figuratively. The feel of his curled tongue darting out to paint her newfound erogenous zone made Melissa gasp with pleasure.

Once his seduction of that territory was completed, he lowered her right leg only to lift her left one and swiftly duplicate his caresses there. Now she had goose bumps all over, although she wasn't the least bit chilled. In fact, she was burning up! Pulses she'd never known she possessed were pounding at her temples, the base of her throat, the juncture of her thighs. She was clenching the sheet when he finally lowered her leg.

He stared at her for a moment, promising her heaven with his eyes even as he took hold of her ankles and pulled her to him until she sat astride his lap. The belt on the silk robe he was wearing had come completely undone, revealing him in all his glory.

"Aspirin," he gasped as she shifted against him with sultry provocation. "We need aspirin!" Shimmying backward, she opened her hand to reveal the condom she had clutched there. Taking it from her, he made quick work of donning its protection before gripping her waist and tugging her to him.

Whispering his name, she guided him home, closing her eyes at the intense satisfaction of finally having him filling her. Moving together, they made slow, sensual love with her perched on his lap, her legs wrapped around his waist. Her head was tilted back in exultant rapture at the ever-increasing spiral of ecstasy. Murmuring dark words of encouragement, Nick leaned forward to kiss the hollow of her throat. With every rocking motion, the bed sheet shifted against them until it eventually slid away entirely, leaving nothing but slick skin gliding against slick skin.

Nick took delight in drawing their lovemaking out. Gasping for breath, they tumbled onto their sides before rolling over the wide expanse of the bed in an abandoned display of passion that had her on top one moment and beneath him the next. It was wild and sweet, passionate and prolonged, exotic and extended.

When the release finally came, it was so powerful that Melissa's entire body pulsated with unadulterated joy. The shudders racking his body conveyed Nick's equal pleasure.

It was some time before either of them could move, let alone speak. Gazing at him, Melissa smiled lazily. "I can't believe we did that." Looking closer, she huskily noted, "You've got blueberry pie all over your chest."

"So do you," he murmured. "Luckily, I know how to fix that." A moment later he lowered his head to lazily lick the sweet fruit filling from her bare skin.

Melissa didn't see how she could be aroused so soon after having just been through the end of the world with him—but she was. Nick took great delight in slowly lapping every bit of blueberry from her tingling body.

"There's no blueberry there!" she gasped as his tongue caressed her intimately.

"It's just as sweet," he assured her, his smile wolfish. Lowering his head, he returned to his wicked seduction. Her ensuing spasms of pleasure were so intense her hips left the bed.

Several moments later, after Melissa was done purring his name and the room was quiet once more, Nick heard something outside the bedroom door. Seconds later, a sound at the door brought Nick to his feet, ready to face an unseen intruder. "What the hell was that?"

Melissa was too breathless to speak. She felt as if every bone in her body had melted. She couldn't even make a fist.

Stalking naked to the door, Nick yanked it open to find Magic lying there, her front paws outstretched. It took him a minute to put things together. The cat must have stuck her paws under the door and rattled it, creating one heck of a racket.

"She doesn't like being locked out," Melissa finally had the energy to say.

Hearing the sound of her mistress's voice, Magic scooted toward the bed, missing it the first time but making a successful jump on her second attempt. Purring, the cat settled on the foot of the bed and stared at Nick with eerie intensity. Before he knew it, he was reaching for the silk robe on the floor.

"Don't worry, she's nearsighted," Melissa told him with a grin.

"You're getting a kick out of this, aren't you?" he grumbled.

"I've gotten enough kicks for one evening," she drawled with sleepy satisfaction. A minute later, she was asleep.

Walking over to the bed, Nick smoothed her hair away from her face. Settling beside her, he pulled the sheet over them both, careful not to dislodge a complaining Magic in the process.

He switched off the bedside lamp, but couldn't switch off his thoughts. Melissa *still* hadn't said she loved him. And he still hadn't decided how they were going to work out the details of having a future together. There simply weren't enough opportunities in Greely for him to make a living as an architect here. And he couldn't see Melissa moving to Chicago. She'd told him herself that she'd hated her time spent in the big city.

What to do—how to solve this dilemma? Nick felt his old insecurities returning. He was no expert at this. Hell, he didn't have a clue how to deal with an issue like love. How to make it work. For that matter, how could he even be sure that Melissa *did* love him?

Nick wrestled with his personal demons long into the night, all too aware that—with only two days left of his vacation—time was running out. And he was running out of options.

Ten

Nick woke to the feel of a warm body at his back. It took him a moment or two to realize the body was small...and was purring. Blearily looking over his shoulder, he saw the tri-colored fur of Melissa's cat. But there was no sign of Melissa. Then he saw the note on the pillow.

Nick—Had to go to work. Didn't want to wake you. Sleep as long as you like. I'll see you later.

Lissa

P.S. Don't let anyone see you when you leave, OK?

Nick crumpled the note in his hand. Startled, Magic jumped at the sound and leapt from the bed, scratching Nick's shoulder as she used it as a launching pad. Muttering, Nick headed for the bathroom.

Staring in the mirror and wiping the blood from his shoulder, he mockingly noted that now he had two scars—

one on his thumb from Lissa and one on his shoulder from her cat. But it was his heart he was worried about. Because Melissa had the power to hurt him there. And that scar wouldn't be a minor injury, it would be fatal. Fatal to his ability to hope, his ability to believe that he'd find happiness in love, that he was worthy of being loved.

If she loves you, why is she so ashamed of you? a little voice inside his head questioned. "She's not ashamed of me," he muttered at his bleary-eyed reflection in the mirror. He hadn't fallen asleep until dawn, and then it was to dream that he was being ridiculed and mocked, as he had been as a child.

Splashing some cold water on his face made him feel better. He wasn't going to let his doubts get the better of him. And he wasn't going to let Melissa get away from him. She was the best thing that had ever happened to him, and he would fight to the end for her—even if it meant fighting his internal demons. And he'd win...win Melissa and her love.

"Did you hear the news?" Mrs. Cantrell asked Melissa in a breathless voice of excitement.

Melissa hoped it wasn't the news that Nick had been caught leaving her house this morning. She'd felt awkward adding that postscript to her note, but what they shared was too special for her to want to share it with the entire population of Greely yet.

It might not be logical, it might not make sense, but Melissa just wanted to keep what they had to herself for a while. To nurture it and secretly cherish it, as she had the doll her mother had given her before she'd left. Melissa had kept it in its special carrying case hidden under her bed—only taking it out at night and hugging it to herself, whispering promises, sharing confidences.

The doll hadn't stayed hidden for long once her father remarried. Her stepmother had found it and given it to her own daughter—telling Melissa that, having just turned nine, she was too old to be playing with dolls. Melissa had fought to keep her treasured Betsy doll to no avail. She'd been spanked and sent to bed for being selfish. And her stepsister had gloated over having the doll that had been Melissa's most treasured possession. But even that hadn't lasted long, as her younger stepsister had soon broken the doll and it had been tossed out before Melissa had known about it.

"Melissa, did you hear a word I said?"

Melissa shook her head, both in answer to Mrs. Cantrell's question and to clear her head of a memory she hadn't thought of in years.

"I asked you if you'd heard the news?" Mrs. Cantrell repeated.

"What news?"

"Wayne and Rosie have had a huge fight. I just came from the Cut N' Curl, and I heard it from Rosie myself. She did a nice job on my cut, don't you think?" Mrs. Cantrell patted her curls. "I told her not to do anything too drastic."

"It looks fine," Melissa absently assured her, her thoughts on the news she'd just heard. So Rosie and Wayne had had a fight? A few weeks ago that news would have been manna to her ears. Now it made no difference. She felt curiously distanced from Wayne. And in a strange way, that unnerved her. Because Melissa had been so sure she'd loved him. So what did that mean about her judgment where love was concerned? Would she love Nick, only to fall out of love with him days later?

The first thing that came to mind was that Nick and Wayne were *nothing* alike. Wayne was all flashy sunlight, easy to like but lacking any real depth. Nick was the darkness of night, hard to decipher and filled with mystery—yet familiar and welcoming to those few who knew their way in the dark, those who felt cloaked by the protective indigo shadows of the night.

No, Melissa wasn't worried that Nick was like Wayne in any way. She was worried about herself, that something was wrong with *her*. Patty had said she deserved to be happy, but at times Melissa wasn't sure that was really true.

Nick was waiting for her at his cabin, where he'd invited her for dinner. He'd cooked burgers out on the grill and had set up a table to go with the two director's chairs on the front porch. He'd suggested eating outside in order to catch the slight breeze off the lake. The purple knit dress she wore, sleeveless with buttons running from collar to hem, was suited to the warm July evening.

To the casual observer it would appear that Melissa and Nick were having a friendly dinner together, nothing more. But Melissa was aware of the undercurrents between them. She could only wonder at the cause.

"Has Alberta been giving you any more trouble?" she asked Nick after they'd finished eating without more than a few sentences having passed between them.

"I haven't seen a flash of her binoculars, if that's what's worrying you."

"I'm not worried."

"Aren't you?" Was it her imagination or did his quiet voice have a new edge to it? Melissa wondered.

"Is something bothering you?" she asked him.

Instead of answering, Nick stared past her shoulder to the rippled surface of the lake. His gaze was one of brooding intensity. Melissa couldn't read anything more than that. Was he regretting the change in their relationship? The new intimacy? Was he feeling smothered? She was afraid to ask those questions, so instead, she whispered, "Nick?"

He returned his gaze and his attention to her. "Let's go for a walk," he said quietly.

Melissa's fingers trembled as he held out his hand for her to take. Oh, God, he wasn't going to dump her, was he? Not Nick.

As if sensing her nervousness, Nick used his free hand to reach out and smooth her hair behind her ear. His fingers lingered to caress the warmth of her cheek. His smile warmed her heart and reassured her soul. The need and desire in his expression were as powerful as ever.

Turning her head, she kissed his fingertips. Whatever was wrong, they'd face it together. But she wouldn't press him. Clearly he didn't want to talk about it now.

Hands clasped, they ambled along the dirt path that edged Moment Lake. Not really a formal path, its existence was only known to those who knew to look for it. They paused now and then to skip a few stones along the way. It became one of those quiet interludes that Melissa so enjoyed with Nick. Like the time she'd spent barefoot on his front porch, or talking in her living room. She never felt this sense of inner contentment with anyone else.

Maybe it was caused by the fact that she wasn't on guard with Nick, not worrying about what he'd think if she said or did something wrong. Acceptance was a powerful thing, and a rare one. The ability to be quiet with someone was just as important as the ability to share secrets with him. Melissa tightened her hold on his hand.

By the time they'd almost completed the walk around the lake, the sun was preparing to set. By mutual consent, they paused to enjoy the fiery display. Melissa had always felt that one of the advantages of living in such flat countryside was seeing so much sky. And sunset brought the sky's canvas to brilliant life—with splashes of yellow, fiery orange and radiant red. High cirrus clouds reflected the pastel colors, coming alive with a glow that mirrored the horizon. Watching the chromatic show made her feel very small, and it recharged the spirit of her soul every time she saw it. They stood there watching until the solar flame was all but extinguished.

After having stared at the brightness lingering on the horizon for so long, they didn't realize how dark it had actually become, and when they resumed their walk, Melissa stumbled on the unlit path.

"The moon will be up soon," Nick murmured, putting his arm around her shoulder to help guide her over the roughness of the dirt path.

As they continued to move in the darkness, Melissa felt the awareness between them growing with every breath she took. Nick had shifted his hold so that his arm was around her waist, his fingers resting on her hip. Every step she took brought a new wave of anticipation. She knew Nick felt it, too, so it came as no surprise when he stopped in his tracks and kissed her.

The passion between them escalated quickly. Like the sunset, it seemed to have been a long time building followed by a sudden burst of glorious beauty. He held her to him as if wanting to imprint the feel of her body. His kiss was all fiery passion and urgent desire, and it set her on fire as surely as a match to dry tinder.

"I want you now," he muttered against her mouth.

Excitement shot through her. "The cabin..."

"Too far away," he growled, kissing her again—deeply, ardently. "I know somewhere else," he promised, as he gently nipped her throat with his teeth before soothing her with his tongue.

Melissa nodded her agreement and seconds later found herself being led beneath the protective covering of a willow tree growing nearby.

Ducking beneath the sheltering fronds, he backed her against the tree trunk, propping his hand above her head as he had that night outside the community center. "I've thought of doing this ever since the square dance," he roughly confessed before leaning down to kiss her once more.

Melissa was no passive participant. She returned his passion with equal ardor, her fingers undoing his shirt as she'd longed to do that night. Whatever his mouth did, she imitated and elaborated upon—nibble for nibble, tongue stroke for tongue stroke.

"I watched you that night," she whispered as he undid the buttons on her dress from collar to hem. "Watched you walking toward me. I wanted you then."

"I wanted to do this then," Nick replied as he bared her breasts to his tender caresses. This time he undid the front fastening on her bra with the triumphant smile of a man confident of his reception.

His hands cupping her breasts were hotter than the sun at high noon, and they burned her with their erotic touch—a blissful burn that kindled flames deep within her. Their lips met again, his tongue thrusting as his hips were. Moving rapidly, he slid his hands up her thighs to peel away her underwear. As Melissa stepped out of it, hastily kicking off her sandals at the same time, she focused her attention on undoing his jeans—sliding them and his underwear out of the way. He donned the protection he had stashed in his jeans pocket.

Opening her dress as if opening a treasured volume, he slid his hands inside to span her bare waist. Pulling her to him, he lifted her, darkly murmuring, "Put your legs around me."

She did, clutching his shoulders as he gave her the ride of her life—coming into her with a surge of raw power. The pleasure was so intense her fingers dug into his shoulders, distantly realizing as she did so that he was still wearing his open shirt. The fact that they were partially dressed and had come together in such a fiery frenzy brought with it a new sense of forbidden pleasure. Gasping his name, she instinctively clenched around his throbbing warmth. Now he was the one to groan and bury his face in her silky hair.

He shifted so that the thick tree trunk supported her, and his hands were free to slide up her body, skimming the sides of her breasts as they were pressed against him. Her nipples thrust against his bare chest. His every move created a friction that was incredibly thrilling.

She felt the roughness of the bark at her back through the protective covering of her knit cotton dress. She felt the warmth of the sultry night air on her bare skin. But most of all she felt Nick, locked to her, surging within her, touching her deepest recesses.

At her next tiny shiver, he groaned even louder and slid his hands down to her bottom as he shifted her and brought her even tighter against him. One more move…and her soul left her body as she soared to the sky, the taut, earthbound rope of anticipation cutting free and rippling through her with dizzying sharpness. The pleasure was so intense she cried out his name.

Later, when she finally came back to earth and her feet returned to the ground, Melissa was shocked at what she'd just done, at how wild she'd been. She hadn't even waited for Nick to remove his jeans. And then for her to scream like that… She held her hands to her hot cheeks.

"I hope no one heard me," she muttered while hastily putting her clothing in order.

Nick paused in the process of fastening his jeans. Her words struck him completely the wrong way, causing his earlier doubts to return tenfold. After the absolutely incredible moment they'd just shared, her first thoughts were concern that someone might have heard? No confession to loving him. No soft tenderness. No, all he saw was shame and embarrassment. Doubts gnawed at his patience. He couldn't keep quiet any longer. "Why should you care if someone heard us or not?" he demanded brusquely.

"Because I don't want it to get all over town that I was making love with you under the willow by Moment Lake."

"Why not?" he angrily shot back. "Are you ashamed of me?"

"Of course not."

"You don't want lover boy hearing about us now that he's free, is that it?"

She looked at him in surprise. "What are you talking about?"

"Wayne. I know that he's broken up with Rosie. That's what this is all about, isn't it?"

"They've had a fight. I don't know that they've broken up."

"Right." Nick angrily stuffed his shirt into the waistband of his jeans. "And you didn't want to burn your bridges with him. After all, should your true love be on the market again, you'd dump me and take up with him in a minute. Well, let me tell you something, I've had it with playing second fiddle to a jerk who jilted you days before your wedding! If you thought you could use me to get over him, you thought wrong."

"I never thought you could make me get over Wayne."
Melissa could tell immediately by the bitter look on his face
that it was the wrong thing to say.

"Oh, right, forgive me for being so bold," he drawled. "I
forgot that *nothing* could make you forget your one true
love."

"That's not what I meant," she protested.

Nick's face was set in granite, the expression in his eyes as
impenetrable as the night surrounding them. "I think we've
both said enough for one night. It's time for us to go back."

Melissa wanted to go back in time and make things right
between them again. But she wasn't sure how. A huge full
moon was just rising over the eastern horizon, lending
enough light for them to quickly return to his cabin. The trip
was made in silence as Melissa struggled to find the right
words to say to Nick. Would he even believe her if she said
she loved him? After all, she'd said she'd loved Wayne a few
weeks ago, told Nick that herself. And did Nick even *want*
her love? After all, he hadn't said he loved her.

When they reached his cabin, he curtly said, "I'll walk
you home."

"No," she instinctively protested, not wanting to leave
while things were so antagonistic between them.

"Right. You don't want anyone seeing me with you. I
know, you've made that much clear. Fine. Have it your
way." Without another word, he turned on his heel and
stalked off, disappearing into the woods bordering the lake.

Melissa barely slept at all that night. Wanting to clear the
air with Nick, she stopped at his cottage on her way to work
the next morning. She would have gone in the middle of the
night, she might as well have since she was up anyway, but
had decided it might be best to let him cool down a little. So
she'd waited until this morning.

His car was parked in the drive, which meant he was home. But as she got out of her compact car, she realized there was a suitcase sitting on the other side of the drive. A second later, Nick emerged from the cabin with a duffel bag in his hand.

"What are you doing?" she asked unsteadily.

"What does it look like I'm doing? I'm leaving. I have to go back to Chicago," he curtly told her. "The firm called me late last night. Something has come up. They need me right away."

I need you, too, Melissa wanted to say, but the words lay lodged in her throat, held there by fear. What if Nick was taking off on her the way Wayne had? What if he'd decided he was tired of having an affair with her and wanted to return to the bright lights of the city? How was a woman like her supposed to hold the attention of a complicated man like him? "I thought you said you didn't want to work in Chicago anymore," she managed to say.

"I've learned that what I want and what I get are two different things," he said wearily.

"Will you be back?"

"That depends on you," he said, his expression still fiercely remote. "While I'm gone, I suggest that you think about who and what you really want. I've had it with waiting around."

"Nick..."

What she was about to say was forever interrupted by his kiss, which was hard and brief and angry. Yet it felt as if he was kissing her goodbye. Before she could get her scattered thoughts together, he was gone, leaving Melissa standing alone in the drive as she was left behind yet again.

"I just saw Nick drive out of town like a bat out of Hades," Patty told Melissa as she stopped by the library a few minutes later.

On the verge of tears, Melissa said, "I think I may have really screwed up."

"What happened?"

"Nick's left. He's gone to Chicago, and I'm not sure he's ever coming back."

"Did you ask him if he was coming back?"

Melissa nodded.

"And what did he say?"

"That it depended on me."

"Then it doesn't sound like he's out-and-out left you, Melissa. What happened? Did you two have a fight?"

Again, Melissa nodded.

"What about?" Patty asked.

"I'm not even sure. It happened so suddenly. He said he was tired of waiting around for me to make up my mind between him and Wayne. That's not what I've been doing," Melissa assured her friend. "I haven't been using Nick to get over Wayne."

"Is that what he accused you of doing?"

"That and more. He said I was ashamed of him because I wasn't willing to parade the fact that we were sleeping together. I just wanted to keep something special to myself for a while. What was so bad about that?"

"Nothing, as long as Nick knew that was the reason you wanted to be discreet. Did you tell him that?"

Melissa shook her head. "He took off before I could."

"You could always call him."

"I don't have his phone number. Oh, God, what if I never hear from him again?"

"Melissa, you're a librarian. Information is your business. I think you could manage to track him down in Chicago, if he doesn't come back on his own. But I think he will. I saw the way he looked at you while you two were dancing. As if you were the moon and the stars rolled into one. And before you say that Wayne once looked at you that

way, too, let me remind you that Wayne and Nick are nothing alike.''

"I know that,'' Melissa murmured.

"Then know he'll come back.''

Melissa hung on to that belief for the first twelve hours.
Nick didn't call her. She told herself she hadn't expected him
to. She told herself she wasn't disappointed. She lied.

It was nearly impossible not to give in to the panic and
despair threatening the edges of her control. Logically she
knew her emotions were being magnified by the fact that she
felt she'd been left—yet again. The other times came back
to haunt her, being left first by her mother when she was
eight, then by her father when he married Vivien and moved
to California, then by Wayne when he jilted her, and now by
Nick. Her emotional reaction to the situation was to cry and
delve into her freezer for ice cream. She spent the first part
of the evening doing just that.

But as Melissa sat on her couch with Magic purring in her
lap, she realized that Nick hadn't really left her like the others had. His last comment kept coming back to her. Would
he be back—that depended on her. Which meant what?
That something she'd said or done had driven him away?

And, boy, did that concept bring a fresh batch of tears!
Because deep down, in a place she'd never examined before, she already blamed herself for all the others leaving
her. Words from the past returned to haunt her, words she'd
overheard as a child when her stepmother had been talking
to her father. "That girl is impossible! She would drive
anyone to distraction,'' Vivien had said. "I can see why your
first wife took off.''

Nick was absolutely right in his recollections of Melissa
having a temper as a child, and it had really come out that
summer after her mother left. But after hearing Vivien's
comment, Melissa had changed—done her best to fit in, to

be a good girl so she wouldn't cause any more trouble. Because if she'd been a good girl in the first place, then her mother wouldn't have left.

Magic meowed in concern at the tears running down Melissa's cheeks. Melissa had toned down her anger, been a "good girl," and Wayne had left her anyway. Which proved what? That love wasn't dependable? That she wasn't worthy of being loved?

Dammit, she *was* worthy! Melissa scrubbed the tears from her face and lifted her chin. She *was* worthy. Nick had taught her that much. And more.

Magic jumped onto the couch pillow beside Melissa, only to pounce on her own tail a second later. The cat's antics reminded Melissa of Independence Day and Nick's Chinese proverb about happiness. Without Nick, Melissa had no happiness. That was a certainty.

It was early afternoon on Saturday when Nick pulled his car to a stop in front of Melissa's house. He rang the bell, pounded on the door. No reply. He was getting ready to peer into the living room window when the Beasley sisters saw him poised on the front steps.

The two sisters paused on the sidewalk to speak to him. "Melissa isn't home," Alberta stated.

"She's at St. Andrew's church," Beatrice said with a fluttery wave of her handkerchief.

"With Wayne," Alberta clearly took pleasure in adding.

"Why would she be at church with Wayne?" Nick demanded.

"Why do you think?" Alberta shot back. "There's a wedding going on. One this town has been waiting for."

Nick paled. And then panicked. Melissa. Wayne. Getting married? No! It couldn't happen! He wouldn't let it! Damn his pride, damn the insecurities that had caused their fight. Cursing himself for giving her that ultimatum before he'd left for Chicago, Nick took off at a run toward the church three blocks away.

"Why did you tell him that?" Beatrice asked her sister.

"He needed to hear the truth," Alberta said. "Bring him to his senses. I think he'll do the right thing now."

"Why, sister, I think that deep down you're a romantic after all," Beatrice noted fondly.

"Bite your tongue," Alberta said sharply, but her gaze was wistful as she watched Nick disappear around the corner.

As Nick ran, he hoped that Alberta had been lying about Melissa and Wayne. But when he reached St. Andrew's, there was a white limo waiting outside the sandstone church. A white limo decorated with wedding paraphernalia. His racing heart sank to his shoes. A wedding *was* taking place!

Praying that he wasn't too late, Nick leapt up the concrete steps leading to the church's entrance and raced across the vestibule to open the heavy wooden door leading to the nave just in time to hear the minister say, "If there is any among you who know why these two should not be lawfully married, let them speak now or forever hold their peace."

Whereupon Nick shouted, "Stop the wedding!"

Eleven

Nick saw the minister's startled expression as he stared at Nick in unnerved dismay. Moments later the bride and groom turned around to face him with equal surprise.

The first thing Nick noticed was that the bride wasn't Melissa. He relaxed muscles that had tensed in preparation for the worst. Melissa wasn't the one marrying this lug head....

Only then did Nick realize that the groom wasn't Wayne.

Scanning the small number of guests in the pews, he wondered if Wayne and Melissa were merely attending the wedding. But, no, he didn't see either of them.

"Sorry," he muttered, his face turning red. "My mistake. Go right ahead with the proceedings. I'm sorry to have interrupted."

Pivoting on his heel, he left as quickly as he'd entered, carefully closing the nave door behind him. After having sprinted those three blocks to get here and then racing into

the church like a madman, Nick needed a moment to catch
his breath. And to collect his chaotic thoughts. He'd only
been gone three days—hardly time for Melissa to have gotten married, if he'd stopped to think about it logically.

But then he couldn't be logical with Melissa. She meant
too much to him. Which is why he'd returned to Greely as
soon as humanly possible, having given his notice to his
employer. Now he had to find Melissa.

Looking up, he saw her standing to one side of the vestibule. From the look on her face, he could tell she'd witnessed at least part of his attempt to stop the wedding taking
place inside. "What are you doing here?" she asked him.

"What are you doing here?" he countered, not in any
hurry to elaborate on how he'd just made a fool of himself.

"I'm organizing the books for the library's book drive.
The sale is tomorrow. Since we don't have any room at the
library, we've been storing the donations in the church
basement. I was down there separating the paperbacks from
the hardcovers," she said, pointing to the stairs behind her.
"What are you doing here?" she repeated.

"Alberta told me you and Wayne were at the church."

"Alberta knew I was here working on the book sale."
Melissa wondered if the elder Beasley sister had sent Nick
racing over here out of vengeance or for some other purpose—namely to reunite Melissa and Nick in a most dramatic way. For some reason, Melissa believed the latter. And
if that had been Alberta's plan, it had certainly worked!

"She said that a wedding was taking place, one the town
had been waiting for," Nick growled.

"That's right," Melissa confirmed. "Wayne *Powalski's*
wedding. Not mine. And certainly not mine to Wayne
Turner. Despite what Wayne might want."

"He wants you back, doesn't he?"

Melissa nodded. In the past two days, Wayne had done his best to convince her to resume their broken engagement. "He and Rosie have broken up."

Nick muttered a curse.

"No, it's the best thing that could have happened," Melissa noted with a slight smile.

Nick froze, feeling as if he'd aged ten years in the past ten minutes. He had his answer. His life and his hope for the future were gone. Darkness without sunshine. Alone. Shut out. Again.

"I knew I loved you before he broke up with Rosie," Nick distantly heard Melissa continue. "But I know you, and you'd have wondered if I only loved you because I couldn't have him. Now you know that's not the case. I *could* have him again if I wanted. I don't. I'm not interested. Not at all."

"Not at all?" Nick repeated, dazed.

"Not at all. What I felt for him is nothing like what I feel for you. I love you. You love me for who I am. I don't have to pretend to be something I'm not."

Nick heard a whistling in his ears and prayed he wasn't going to pass out on the vestibule floor. Melissa took his arm and led him over to a wooden bench against the wall. "Are you all right?" she asked, her voice husky with concern.

"Start again at the beginning," he muttered.

"With what are you doing here?"

"After that."

"I love you," she softly repeated. She watched as he closed his eyes, the tenseness in his lean face replaced with relief.

"I did a lot of thinking while you were gone, you know," she confessed. "About a lot of things. And I discovered that the reason I really became engaged to Wayne is that he became my passport to respectability. I wanted the life he represented. Not the *material* things he represented. Wayne's not wealthy by any stretch of the imagination. I mean, the security I thought he offered. Like I said, the respectability. But now I realize I'm respectable all on my own. I don't need Wayne to give me that."

"That's right," Nick said, his pride in her apparent in his quiet voice and his green eyes.

"I'm my own woman," she said with some measure of awe at the discovery. "Not the daughter of the scandalous hussy who ran off with the postmaster twenty-some years ago, not the fiancé of the popular football coach who was jilted days before her wedding."

"What made you finally reach this realization?"

"You did," she said unsteadily, reaching out to tenderly touch his cheek. "*You* did," she repeated.

"What did I do?"

"Made me believe in myself. That was your intention, and it worked. *Finally,*" she added with a grin. "I'm only sorry it took so long. But you see, things got mixed up in my mind."

Pressing her hand to his face, he murmured, "What things?"

"Things to do with my childhood. When you left three days ago, you said that whether or not you came back depended on me."

"I shouldn't have—"

She shifted her hand to his mouth, stopping his words. "Yes, you should have. Because it made me face a few things. Like the fact that I'd been holding myself responsible for my mother leaving all those years ago. And then when she was killed in a car accident a few years later, there was no way of asking her about it myself."

"You never told me she was dead." Nick lowered her hand from his face to encompass it in his, threading his fingers through hers. "Why would you think you were responsible for her leaving?"

"Because when I was a kid, I overheard my stepmother say it. That I was the reason my mother left. That I was impossible."

Nick muttered something dark and threatening under his breath, none of it complimentary to her stepmother.

"Then I started thinking about it...and you know...my father...well, he isn't exactly the most loving man around," Melissa admitted. "I can understand better now why my mother needed to leave him. I'll never know why she didn't take me with her, but I no longer think that I was to blame for her leaving."

"You *weren't* to blame," Nick declared emphatically.

"I didn't know that at the time. My stepmother claimed that I would drive anyone away. Remember my temper that summer my mom left?"

"I remember it saving my hide on more than one occasion," he dryly noted. "You had spirit, Lissa. And you'd had a rough time, what with your mother leaving."

"After that summer I tried to fit in with my father's new family. Really I did."

"I'm sure you did. Tried to fit in by killing your own spirit."

"But it didn't work. I was never part of that family. And I never will be. Which is why I so wanted to have a family of my own. And that's what I saw in Wayne. I did everything I thought I was supposed to. I was a 'good girl,' and it made no difference in the end. Wayne left me, just as everyone else had."

"So you felt like an outcast," Nick astutely noted. "A misfit."

"We have that in common, don't we?" Melissa replied.
"You grew up the same way, feeling as if you weren't part
of your family."

Nick nodded.

"Not knowing what it was to be loved," she continued.

"I can't believe anyone not loving you," he murmured
softly. "I wish I'd been here to slay your dragons for you.
Particularly that dragon of a stepmother."

"You've taught me that I'm strong enough to slay my
own dragons . . . with your support. In the end, I took your
advice, you know."

"What advice?"

"I'm living life for myself, doing what will make *me*
happy. And you make me happy, Nick. Happier than I've
ever been in my life."

"Same here," he said huskily. "I've been a loner most of
my life. I've never needed anyone else, never thought I was
cut out to have anyone love me."

"Oh, Nick, you deserve to be loved. I've never met a man
more deserving."

"Still trying to pin that knight-in-shining-armor image on
me?" he inquired wryly.

"You're my champion. Just as I am yours. And you're
my friend. Just as I am yours. So you do dumb things
sometimes, like storming off to Chicago," she said with an
irreverent grin. "I do dumb things, too, sometimes, like
getting engaged to Wayne. I'm just thankful that I found
you in the end."

"You and I both. When I think what could have happened if I hadn't come back to Greely this summer . . ." He
tightened his hold on her hand.

"We were meant to be together. Must be fate."

"Speaking of fate, you won't believe what happened
when I returned to Chicago," Nick said. "An old college

buddy of mine had been trying to get in touch with me. Seems he heard about a position he thought I might be interested in. In the state capital.''

"Springfield is a two-hour drive from here."

"It's closer than Chicago is," Nick pointed out. "And I'd be working with a foundation that does historic preservation work. Protecting old buildings instead of knocking them down."

"You went to jail once to protect a building," she reminded him.

"That was a long time ago. And I lost myself in the interim. But now I'm back on track. I've also gotten some interest in specialized projects, which I could work on from here. Free-lance work, not the steadiest of jobs by any means. But with a computer and a fax modem I can set up an office here. My buddy reminded me that the cost of living in a small town is much less than it is in Chicago. With the part-time work in Springfield and the free-lance stuff, I'll be able to make enough to get by. It won't be anything close to what I made in Chicago, though."

"Does that bother you?" she asked him.

"I'm more worried about it bothering you."

"What, do I look like I stepped out of 'Lifestyles of the Rich and Famous'?" she demanded mockingly. In a more serious tone of voice, she said, "I'd rather you were happy than rich, Nick."

"You're one of a kind."

"So are you. But you are forgetting one thing."

"What?"

"You still haven't said you love me."

"Of course I love you! I think I always have. I *know* I always will."

A second later she was in his arms, where she was meant to be. His lips met hers in a kiss of reunion that expressed a newfound faith in happy endings in addition to a wonderfully passionate hunger. Melissa felt whole again for the first time since they'd had their argument three days ago. Nick filled the hollowness in her soul with his outpouring of love. His having said the words aloud made this physical expression all the more moving and all the more satisfying.

His mouth brushed hers with slow, reverent strokes as he held her to him as if unable to believe she was real. Melissa recognized the feeling, for she was experiencing the same thing as she ran her fingers through his dark wavy hair. It was as if only by touching him could she reaffirm that this truly was happening, that they really were together again, and would stay that way forever more.

Their tender embrace was finally interrupted by the hubbub of the newlyweds running from the church amid a shower of rice.

Taking Melissa by the hand, Nick tugged her to her feet. "Come on."

"Where are we going?"

"To talk to the minister about setting a date for *our* wedding!"

Concerned by her stunned expression, it occurred to Nick that she might not want a church wedding after the disaster with Wayne. Looking at her uncertainly, he murmured, "Unless you'd rather just elope?"

Her smile was as brilliant as a downstate sunset. "I don't care what we do, as long as we do it together."

"Then let's go talk to that minister."

Nick and Melissa walked outside just in time for the floral bouquet the bride had thrown to land smack in the middle of Nick's chest.

"Nice catch," Melissa said with a grin.

"She taught me everything I know," Nick told the laughing crowd before handing the bouquet to Melissa. For her ears only, he softly added, "You taught me everything I know about love."

Melissa had no words to express the happiness in her heart. She'd found the perfect cure for the bridal blues. True love.

* * * * *

COMING NEXT MONTH

#895 AN OBSOLETE MAN—Lass Small
December's *Man of the Month*, rugged Clinton Terrell, had only
sexy Wallis Witherspoon on his mind. So he trapped her on a ranch,
determined to make this irresistible intellectual *his!*

#896 THE HEADSTRONG BRIDE—Joan Johnston
Children of Hawk's Way
When rancher Sam Longstreet hoodwinked curvaceous Callen Whitelaw
into marrying him, he had only wanted revenge. But it didn't take long
before he was falling for his headstrong bride!

#897 HOMETOWN WEDDING—Pamela Macaluso
Just Married!
Callie Harrison vowed to marry bad boy Rorke O'Neil years ago, but
she bailed out before the wedding. Now Rorke was back with a secret—
one Callie might not be able to forgive....

#898 MURDOCK'S FAMILY—Paula Detmer Riggs
When divorced Navy SEAL Cairn Murdock's family was threatened, he
raced to their sides. Nothing, not even the burning secret he held, would
prevent him from keeping the woman he'd never stopped loving safe....

#899 DARK INTENTIONS—Carole Buck
Sweet Julia Kendricks decided to help Royce Williams adjust to life in
darkness after he lost his eyesight. But soon *he* was helping *her* see his
true intentions....

#900 SEDUCED—Metsy Hingle
Michael Grayson didn't need love, but he *did* need a wife, in order to
keep custody of his niece. So he seduced sophisticated Amanda Bennett,
never expecting to fall for the fiery woman....

**Another wonderful year of romance
concludes with**

Christmas
Memories

Share in the magic and memories of romance
during the holiday season with this collection of two
full-length contemporary Christmas stories,
by two bestselling authors

**Diana Palmer
Marilyn Pappano**

Available in December at your favorite retail outlet.

Only from   Silhouette®

™   **where passion lives.**

XMMEM

JINGLE BELLS, WEDDING BELLS:
Silhouette's Christmas Collection for 1994

Christmas Wish List

*To beat the crowds at the malls and get the perfect present for *everyone,* even that snoopy Mrs. Smith next door!

*To get through the holiday parties without running my panty hose.

*To bake cookies, decorate the house and serve the perfect Christmas dinner—just like the women in all those magazines.

*To sit down, curl up and read my Silhouette Christmas stories!

Join *New York Times* bestselling author Nora Roberts, along with popular writers Barbara Boswell, Myrna Temte and Elizabeth August, as we celebrate the joys of Christmas—and the magic of marriage—with

JINGLE
BELLS,
WEDDING
BELLS

Silhouette's Christmas Collection for 1994.

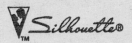

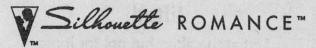
Silhouette ROMANCE™

'Tis the season for romantic bliss.
It all begins with just one kiss—

UNDER THE MISTLETOE

Celebrate the joy of the season and the thrill of romance with this special collection:

#1048 ANYTHING FOR DANNY by Carla Cassidy—Fabulous Fathers
#1049 TO WED AT CHRISTMAS by Helen R. Myers
#1050 MISS SCROOGE by Toni Collins
#1051 BELIEVING IN MIRACLES by Linda Varner—Mr. Right, Inc.
#1052 A COWBOY FOR CHRISTMAS by Stella Bagwell
#1053 SURPRISE PACKAGE by Lynn Bulock

Available in December, from Silhouette Romance.

SRXMAS

Jilted!

Left at the altar, but not for long.

Why are these six couples
who have sworn off love
suddenly hearing wedding bells?

Find out in these scintillating books
by your favorite authors,
coming this November!

#889   **THE ACCIDENTAL BRIDEGROOM**
        by Ann Major
        (Man of the Month)

#890   **TWO HEARTS, SLIGHTLY USED**
        by Dixie Browning

#891   **THE BRIDE SAYS NO**
        by Cait London

#892   **SORRY, THE BRIDE HAS ESCAPED**
        by Raye Morgan

#893   **A GROOM FOR RED RIDING HOOD**
        by Jennifer Greene

#894   **BRIDAL BLUES**
        by Cathie Linz

Come join the festivities when six handsome
hunks finally walk down the aisle...

only from

SILHOUETTE® Desire®

JILT

"HOORAY FOR HOLLYWOOD" SWEEPSTAKES

HERE'S HOW THE SWEEPSTAKES WORKS

OFFICIAL ENTRY COUPON

"Hooray for Hollywood"
SWEEPSTAKES!

Yes, I'd love to win the Grand Prize — a vacation in Hollywood —
or one of 500 pairs of "sunglasses of the stars"! Please enter me
in the sweepstakes!

This entry must be received by December 31, 1994.
Winners will be notified by January 31, 1995.

Name _____

Address _____ Apt. _____

City _____

State/Prov. _____ Zip/Postal Code _____

Daytime phone number _____
(area code)

Account # _____

Return entries with invoice in envelope provided. Each book
in this shipment has two entry coupons — and the more
coupons you enter, the better your chances of winning!

DIRCBS